IVAN THE TERRIBLE GOES ON A FAMILY PICNIC

I0633524

CHARLES HOLDEFER

Sagging
Meniscus

Set in Sabon with LaTeX.

ISBN: 978-1-963846-00-3 (paperback)
ISBN: 978-1-963846-01-0 (ebook)
Library of Congress Control Number: 2024939916

Sagging Meniscus Press
Montclair, New Jersey
saggingmeniscus.com

I saw a highway of diamonds and nobody on it.

B.D.

Contents

The New Garden   3

Deadball   9

Gertie and the Babe   35

Heaven   43

Little Boy and the Carp   49

Antennae   55

Foul   67

Wild West Show   91

The Promise   115

Antediluvian   135

IVAN THE TERRIBLE GOES ON A FAMILY PICNIC

ONE

Outskirts of Pskov, 1569

The New Garden

In a clearing beside a stand of birch trees, Ivan the Terrible surveyed a bubbling cauldron of rabbits and waited for his son, Fyodor the Not So Bad, to stop talking. When would he shut up?

"You see, Father, a man in your position needs a pastime. Enough burning and destruction! The people yearn to come together and play. Let bells ring throughout the kingdom to proclaim a new dispensation!"

What was he supposed to say to that?

A moment later, his grandson, Jerry Who Was Rather Fond of Gardening, trotted into the clearing. He approached them with a yellowing fern and tossed it into the cauldron.

"What's that?" Ivan asked.

"Nilsfoot. It tenderizes and adds sweetness."

Jerry seemed a smart lad, but he was more interested in herbs and spices when he should be paying attention to poisons. He was quick and well-built—subtle, too, unlike his father whose brain was a cow-pat—but, for all his assets, the boy took too much for granted. Did he really think he could become Prince of Livonia at no cost? There were enemies everywhere. Didn't he know that you had to sniff out treason, and sweep it away without mercy? Maybe he'd fallen under the influence of his mother, Sonia Who Was a Woman.

"Father, the people would love you," Fyodor continued. "With your discipline, you could become a saint."

Ivan lifted his eyes to the trees, their trembling leaves; his fingers clenched and unclenched. His son was unbearable when he tried to flatter.

Once, many years ago, when he was his grandson's age, he'd driven a sharp-pointed stake into the chest of a boyar. The man had been insolent. The stake had entered as easily as penetrating a honeycomb, and the twitching of limbs had been surprisingly brief, but the man's face, his startled expression, had changed slowly, very slowly. From disbelief to unhappiness to imploring to resignation—and then, with a bubble of blood in the corner of his mouth, acceptance. Even a sort of relief. The man had learned. The bubble popped and the light faded from his eyes. Ivan had waited, clutching the stake, maintaining leverage, observing each stage. It was not without interest.

But now he couldn't bear to look at Fyodor who, Ivan sensed, was incapable of such transitions towards knowledge.

I am growing old, Ivan thought. I no longer have such patience.

"Father?" Fyodor asked.

Ivan ignored him and turned to his grandson. "Show me your garden."

It wasn't far. Leaving Fyodor the Not So Bad to tend the fire, they left the clearing and made their way along a stream until they came to a place where stones protruded and the current flowed swiftly. Jerry Who Was Rather Fond of Gardening stepped nimbly over the stones and continued up the opposite bank without once looking over his shoulder at his grandfather.

Ivan followed.

Sonia Who Was a Woman had spoken approvingly of her son's latest project. "He spends hours working on it. I've never seen him so excited! It's lovely. He's enlisted the help of sheep." It sounded like foolish talk. Gibberish.

But when they came over a rise, he saw it: a luminous green sward, closely cropped, stretching all the way to an ancient apple orchard, now in blossom. He stopped, turning his head to take it in.

"Here we are!" Jerry called. "Come and see!"

The plot contained a large square, beyond which was a semi-circle. In the center of the square was a mound of dirt.

Was someone buried there? Ivan wondered.

Strangest of all was the grass. For, with the exception of dirt tracks defining the square, it was *all* grass. Nothing a person could eat. Could you even call this place a garden?

"This way, Grandfather."

Jerry climbed onto the pile of dirt.

Warily, Ivan stepped onto the mound.

"Wait here. I'll be right back."

He ran off while Ivan stood under the open sky, wondering why he was wasting a glorious spring day with his daft family instead of attending to his responsibilities. Eventually Jerry Who Was Rather Fond of Gardening returned, wielding a thick stake in one hand, while in the other he carried a bucket.

"Boy, what are you contriving?"

Jerry put down the bucket, which was full of stones.

"Now we can start."

"But how?" Ivan snapped. "Is that what you plant in your square? *Stones?*"

"No. Face that way." He pointed to the corner. "See, it's a diamond."

Jerry ran to the corner, taking his stake. "The stones are for you," he called. "I'll stand here. Now you grab a stone. Throw it at me."

Ridiculous! But it was all so irritating that Ivan obliged him. He hurled a stone, and his grandson dodged it. He hurled another, and to his astonishment, the boy swung the stake and hit it squarely. *Crack!* The stone shot straight back at Ivan who ducked to let it pass. Enraged, he reached into the bucket and seized another stone, taking aim.

This time, the boy smacked it and sent it soaring over the entire garden, beyond the bordering semi-circle, and into the apple trees. Jerry threw back his head and laughed as he ran around his grandfather, touching each corner of the diamond, before returning to where he'd started.

Ivan reached into the bucket for another stone.

"What is the point of this?" he demanded.

Picking up his stake, his grandson called, "People will have a lot of fun with it in the future."

"The future?"

Now Fyodor and Sonia appeared from the stream behind the garden. They carried baskets. She threw a blanket on the ground and took out some plates. Fyodor reached into his basket and extracted a long rabbit. He tore off a leg, and dropped the rest on a plate. He waved and then took a bite.

Outrageous! Ivan thought.

But he picked out another stone, licked his fingers, and flung it with all his might.

TWO

Buford County, 1899

Deadball

I.

Harlan Atkins walked down the street with his heart full of love for all creation. The smell of summer air, the glistening flank of a passing horse. How noble everything appeared! A dog trotted by, ears erect, busy dogging, and Harlan thought: Magnificent! The very incarnation of dogness.

Harlan was on his way to the Morgantown baseball field, and now he looked down into his hand and imagined the face of Fanny Schmidt. Her dark eyes and light red hair, the finest strands of copper. Whenever he wanted to admire her, all he had to do was study his palm and watch her image take form there. Look: there she was! Better, more real than a photograph.

He whispered, "My darling, we'll take our love into the world." He brought his hand to his lips.

Johnny Wales saw him. Loitering in front of the tavern and wearing a ripped shirt and cast-off boots without laces, he watched with curiosity. Harlan noticed Johnny and jerked his hand back, for this was personal. He flicked his wrist, tried to turn his gesture into a wave.

Johnny Wales smiled and blew Harlan a kiss, too.

"Spare change?" he asked.

Johnny could be mean and obscene, Harlan knew, or utterly abject and obsequious. He'd sniffed a lot of turpentine and sometimes slept in the rail yard under a coal car. Most of his teeth were gone, his pants stank, and the skin on the backs of his hands peeled off in bright pink flecks. He was a Legion of distress.

Harlan realized that he couldn't give him a penny or a nickel. Today, all he had on his person was a silver dollar, a gift from his parents, Stephen and Eunice Atkins, the town doctor and the organist for the Methodist Church. So when he approached Johnny—his blotched face, his blackened gums—Harlan pressed the heavy coin in his hand.

Johnny looked up, bewildered.

"Bless you," said Harlan.

II.

Fanny Schmidt was worried about Harlan. Last night he'd spoken to her in a state of exaltation. He was happy, positively aglow, and she was glad for him, but his attitude made her nervous, too. They'd been kissing in the narrow alley behind the store when he pulled away.

"We're embraced by a greater love," he said. "Can't you feel it?"

She liked his arms around her; now she blinked. "I feel lots of things."

"But this is the most important, Fanny."

Ever since he'd heard a preacher a few days ago, he couldn't stop talking this way. He was very sweet but he seemed jumpy and his mind was elsewhere.

She was aware of much unsaid between them, of the fact that Harlan knew little of Fanny's life before her lucky break of landing a job at Goodwin's Variety Store. Fanny had drudged on her father's farm, cooked for her brothers, walked the pastures, pulling cockleburs: the work was endless. Now, in town, life was finer. She stood behind a counter and sold fabric by the yard, salt toffee and lemon drops. Every day brought new people and possibilities.

Best of all, on the wall facing the counter, there was a shelf of books. Fanny eyed them hungrily. She'd resolved to read every one. Simply looking at their spines, the different colors, gave Fanny a shiver of pleasure.

Her employer, Mrs. Goodwin, let her borrow these volumes after business hours as long as she brought them back in pristine condition. In her room at night Fanny copied out verses so she could memorize them and recite them to herself at work the following day.

> *What is it men in women do require?*
> *The lineaments of Gratified Desire.*
> *What is it women do in men require?*
> *The lineaments of Gratified Desire.*

III.

Doctor Stephen and Eunice Atkins were worried about Harlan. They'd discussed their son at breakfast. "He'll get through it," she said. "Won't he?

"Of course," said the Doctor. "It's just a passing stage. Come September, he'll move on to other things."

It wasn't the first time they'd reassured each other with the prospect of Harlan leaving Morgantown. Recently, the young man had professed feelings for a local shop girl. She was in no way appropriate. Their son was supposed to start university in the fall. He was in no position for attachments—especially with that sort of girl.

"I've never seen him in such a state," Eunice said.

"He's discovering life. He has to learn."

Although the Doctor didn't say so to his wife, he privately accused his son of a lack of imagination. What was the matter with him? He should show some spark. The Doctor remembered his own college days, which had included drunkenness and frivolous reading. He'd gambled at cards, consorted with Negroes, and conducted what he now thought of as "venereal research." He'd never discussed these matters with his wife and certainly felt no compunction to mention them to his son, for he'd assumed that the boy would, as boys did, seek out such things for himself. All this was part of the seasoning process to become a man, a man who could return to Morgantown and be trusted as a guarantor for the community, a man whose virtue was informed by experience, not by callow enthusiasm. Getting Harlan out of the clutches of some country wench was one thing; but this latest problem, which arose after a religious revival meeting, was more slippery, since it involved not the flesh but the spirit.

"Anyway," he continued, "our family has never gone in for that kind of soul butter."

"You think so?"

He could see that she was not convinced. He stood up and excused himself.

"I'm going out to the garden."

"Good luck," she told him.

The Doctor assumed a brave face. Each morning before reporting to his office he went behind the house and tended his rows of tomatoes and sugar peas. He enjoyed hoeing in the coolness of the day, a pleasant time in the company of himself. But lately he'd been plagued by uninvited visitors: an invasion of moles.

Burrowing and digging, they'd left his garden and nearby orchard pocked with craters. He'd seen nothing like it. Conventional solutions, such as poisons and traps, had failed. The blind destruction continued, and was even expanding. They despoiled what was his.

"You'll see. I'm not through with you yet."

The Doctor had faith in his powers. Reading up on the creatures, he'd been fascinated to learn that moles were hemophiliacs. If you pricked a mole, it would bleed to death.

So now the Doctor experimented with sharp objects, seeding the holes in his property with nails and broken glass. He walked with a bucket, sprinkling liberally. Each opening gaped like a mouth which he fed. Then he returned to close it up again, patting the surface smooth with the back of a spade.

IV.

Harlan had visited the Love Tabernacle out of boredom. There wasn't much distraction in Morgantown, so you took what you could get. Previously, he'd attended lectures on The Future of Electricity or the Wonders of the Amazon; he'd seen tent shows with turbaned magicians and, of course, traveling circuses. Generally he'd avoided revival meetings because his parents, as solid Methodists, disapproved of shouting and writhing and babbling tongues. If some locals took interest in these displays (generally people on the north side who worked the coal mines alongside Italians and Bohemians and other papists), well, that was their affair. But the Atkins did not dignify these occasions with their presence.

Harlan went to the Love Tabernacle with his buddy Cornelius. They'd walked along with hands in their pockets, discussing baseball. Next week the town team, for which they both played, would face a visiting squad called the Mungo Clowns. It promised to be fun but it was also a source of pressure, since these traveling shows, in addition to antics and costumes, always included players of real talent, ex-professionals who would do their best to create a laugh at your expense. It was important that the local team make a respectable showing in front of the home folks. The Love Tabernacle had pitched its tent on the baseball field, where the grass was still wet and spongy from an afternoon thunderstorm. As they drew near Harlan could see that this event was a paltry affair: a primitive set-up, just a canvas roof on poles. A handful of attendees sat on backless benches in the open air.

"I dunno," said Cornelius doubtfully. "Should we go back?"

Before Harlan could reply, a voice called out, "Come, friends! Come!"

Sheepishly they approached and claimed seats on a rear bench.

The proceedings were not what Harlan expected. The preacher introduced himself as Wilbur Wilson, and he also presented his wife, Rosalie, and his son Davey, who moved on crutches and took a place on a wooden chair. Both Cornelius and Harlan eyed Davey closely, wondering if later in the evening they would witness his healing. Would he throw away his crutches and dance? If Davey was faking his infirmity for the sake of the show, he was pretty good at it, because in addition to his hobble he displayed a twisting twitch in his face and a fishlike wriggle in his shoulders, so you had to wonder how much he was controlling it.

"Are you ready for the love?"

Wilbur Wilson didn't shout, he didn't gesticulate. Pressing his hands together, he spoke in a steady voice about his belief in the Love Tabernacle. He began by describing his past. His father had volunteered for the Union in the Twenty-Third Infantry, in whose service he had died. His mother, beset by mental woes and penury, had sent Wilbur and his brother to the Orphan Home in Glenwood. "That was the loneliest place. Seven years I was there. On a cold February morning of my first year, my brother fell through pond ice and drowned. After that I had nobody. Words cannot describe the solitary desperation of my soul. When I finally left the Orphan Home, I was full of anger and my life had no purpose, and I committed bad acts. Criminal acts. Surely I would've ended up in prison—another very lonely place—if I hadn't met Rosalie, who pulled me out of emptiness and wrath, and revealed to me the Love Tabernacle."

Wilbur began to recite the Beatitudes, which Harlan had heard many times in Sunday school. "*Blessed are the merciful, for they shall obtain mercy.*" Tonight, as fireflies popped here and there in the early evening air, the words sounded less mysterious than usual. They were matter-of-fact, in this man's soothing voice.

Next came the music. Rosalie sang in a soft contralto, Wilbur backed her hoarsely, clapping to keep rhythm, while Davey blew into a wooden flute. One of the boy's wrists curled awkwardly inward but he used it to press the instrument against his breast while his able hand managed to finger the holes. The notes came out true and fine.

"*Count your blessings,*
Name them one by one . . ."

Suddenly Harlan felt himself breathing faster. He'd never cared for the music at the Methodist church, which was no reflection on his mother's organ playing, but somehow the hymns and the instrument sounded distant and grandiloquent and as thick as gravy. Whereas this music—Harlan's throat involuntarily tightened—felt vital. Watching Davey play, he thought how tough it must be to be trapped in his body, while maybe the boy possessed a brilliant brain; or was it the opposite, Davey was slow, on top of his other troubles, which would be awfully tough, too, wouldn't it? But before Harlan could speculate about which predicament was worse, the music carried him along with its beauty, and he felt himself blinking back tears.

After the song, Wilbur Wilson resumed talking. He described how the Love Tabernacle had transformed his life, and how, as he and Rosalie and Davey traveled from town to town, they'd had the joy of sharing it with others. "It's my personal hope that one day I might also find my mother. Since she left me at the Orphan Home, I've had no news, no trace. But she might still be alive and residing in your town. I do not know. She might come to see our Tabernacle, and I could meet her again and embrace her, and comfort her, because everything is going to be all right. Yes, everything is going to be all right." Wilbur paused and slowly passed his eyes over the people present. "I don't think she's here tonight. But I still know joy. Because we are each other's family."

Then he repeated, one more time, the Beatitudes. Harlan felt a clenching in his chest. On this second occasion, the phrases seemed transformed beyond the newly matter-of-fact. Now the words were luminous.

" '*Blessed are the poor in spirit.*' You know, sometimes folks think those words are intended for somebody else. They say to themselves, 'that's for people in distress. Lucky for me, I'm doing fine.' But you know what I think, friends? There are people who are poor in spirit and they don't even know it. They don't realize what they're missing. They, too, need to live in the Love Tabernacle."

And then came the part that Harlan had been dreading with all his heart. Oh, he'd known it was coming! Although Wilbur Wilson hadn't thundered at his listeners or threatened hellfire, or struck his fist on his breast or pointed his finger, there had been moments (Harlan was certain!) when Wilbur was sneaking glances at him. *Why is he looking at me?* he wondered. *What does he see?* In these glances there was something like recognition. Now Wilbur extended a public invitation:

"Maybe you, too, want to live in the Love Tabernacle. Do you feel it in your heart? Are you ready to accept, in its fullness, this gift of grace?"

Harlan's knees began to shake. He couldn't stop them, though he longed to. It was embarrassing, but something gripped him and his desire was undeniable. It would be a lie to pretend otherwise. If he pretended, then whatever else followed would fall short of honesty. *I would not be me.*

"The Love Tabernacle is free to everyone. Its arms are open."

No longer trembling, Harlan found his feet and walked boldly to the front, where he received Wilbur's blessing. Though he was the first to come forward, he was soon joined by a sniffling old woman and a red-faced farm boy. After another song from Rosalie, the meeting came to an end and Wilbur passed the hat. Harlan turned out his pocket and found 15 cents. It was all he had; his other money was at home. The collection this evening, from this small audience, was meagre—instead of coin, one woman offered two eggs—but Wilbur and Rosalie and Davey thanked everyone graciously.

Then it was over and time to leave.

"You all right?" Cornelius asked as they walked across the baseball field.

His friend looked at him askance, but Harlan didn't care.

"You know, these people are serious. They're the real thing."

"Well, they're different, I'll give you that much." Cornelius glanced over his shoulder. "You think they really live on that wagon?"

Harlan observed the silhouettes of a long wagon and two horses nibbling on the outfield grass. Wilbur was taking down the Tabernacle with a special hooked stick, detaching the canvas roof from the poles. A kerosene lamp cast a circle of light. Rosalie moved in and out of the periphery. Davey sat on his chair while a small white dog, which must've been tied up during the meeting, frisked at his feet.

"I'm going to talk to them," Harlan said.

"You sure?"

"Come along, if you like."

Cornelius walked on. "See you tomorrow."

When Harlan returned to the Wilsons, Wilbur was rolling up the canvas while Rosalie put out plates on a rickety wooden table. They hadn't had their supper yet.

"I just want to thank you," Harlan said.

Rosalie turned to him and smiled; Davey leaned forward in his chair. Wilbur straightened, rubbing his hands on his back. For a moment he was silent, then he nodded as if they shared an understanding. "That's not necessary, son. You know where gratitude belongs. It's bigger than any of us, right?"

"Right."

He came forward and squeezed Harlan's shoulder. "I'm glad for you. Tonight you entered the Love Tabernacle. And tomorrow? And the day after? You know where to find it."

With a sudden movement Wilbur lifted his arm and seemed to be pointing at a spot beyond the ballfield, maybe the buildings of Morgantown, or to somewhere further on the horizon. Harlan wasn't sure.

V.

The Doctor fussed with his spade, breathing soft curses at the moles, while his wife spied on him from an upstairs window. Eunice was anxious because she knew their son better than her husband did. And there were facts from the past that she hadn't shared.

Leaving the window, she went to a bureau and opened the bottom drawer and extracted a rectangular object wrapped in cheesecloth. Carefully she unfolded the cloth. Here was her commonplace book, a scrap album and accidental diary containing poems she'd written as a child, pressed violets and signed dance cards from young men before her marriage. There was a lock of hair from little Ruth, Harlan's elder sister, who'd died of diphtheria at the age of three. (The powers of the Doctor had failed utterly and not a day passed that Eunice didn't ache to hold Ruthie, one more time, in her arms.) She turned the pages to the back of the book which was stuffed with early family photographs and daguerreotypes.

There—that one.

Her great-uncle Jakob. The eyes, the nose, even the cast of mouth—the resemblance was astonishing. Exactly like Harlan. You could say it *was* Harlan, but for the wide-bow cravat which was out of style nowadays, the hair swept back from his temples.

According to family accounts, Jakob had been a man of childlike qualities, a mystic, not interested, upon his arrival in America, in helping his brothers at their sawmill. Instead he pursued his inner lights and was remembered chiefly for a single incident: one day, without so much as a goodbye or a word advising the family about his intentions, he'd wandered off into the woods and disappeared. Days passed. Everyone worried, fearing an accident had befallen him. Had he stumbled into a crevasse, or crossed paths with an angry bear? Search parties found no traces, and when everyone was ready to give up, a rumor drifted back to the family about a strange white man who lived with the local Keokuk Indians. One of Jakob's brothers set out with an extra horse to go and fetch him, and upon arriving in the Keokuk village and making inquiries, he was pointed to a particular dwelling, out of which Jakob emerged, chin in the air, belligerent. He steadfastly refused to go home; he said he preferred to live where he was. (Peering out of the dim entrance to the dwelling was the small round face of a young Keokuk woman.) So the brother turned his horses around and went home, his mission a failure. The family grieved the loss of Jakob but went on with their lives, reminding themselves that Jakob had never been much use around the sawmill, anyway. Then, about a year later, early one morning there was a pounding at the door. When they opened, there stood two Keokuk men, with a long-haired Jakob between them. Please, they asked, would the family take him back?

They told Jakob's father that they were tired of him, tired of his talk about his God and of the bad luck that they were convinced Jakob had brought them, for half their village had died of coughing sickness since his arrival. These emissaries, thin and haggard, didn't look too well themselves.

So that was how Jakob returned to the family fold. He still wasn't much of a worker; he retreated to a little white shed and remained a bachelor for the rest of his life. He took a vow of silence which he often broke, because he had many opinions (yet he always renewed the vow, because he believed what he said). The surviving daguerreotype showed a gaunt man in black Sunday dress; in his hands he was clasping a kitten. Jakob's fixed gaze and expression appeared peaceful, though maybe a little distracted. The kitten's eyes bugged out: probably Jakob was squeezing it too hard.

VI.

Was Fanny Schmidt in love with Harlan? She felt she ought to be, she knew that people believed she was lucky to have attracted the attentions of such a prominent young man in the community. Other girls might envy her. But everything was happening so fast.

Her employer, Mrs. Goodwin, had advised her, "You have to watch every step you make, you can't compromise, girl. Fact is, most folks is vicious." She nodded at the jar of lemon drops on the counter. "Every child will steal. And that's just the beginning."

Mrs. Goodwin also counselled Fanny on her appearance, how to pin instead of braid her hair, how to knot her smock at the bust. She looked Fanny up and down. "Oh, you'll do just fine."

Her employer kept a close eye on everyone who crossed the threshold. When a local loafer called Catfish came in the store and tried on all the used eyeglasses in the basket (he never bought anything but he wanted to sidle up to Fanny), Mrs. Goodwin was curt and got rid of him.

But when Harlan Atkins walked in, the reception was different. The first time, he'd come to inquire about mustard seed for his mother. "It's for pickling spice." Mrs. Goodwin introduced him to Fanny and kept the conversation going for twenty minutes. Harlan was nice-looking, with solid shoulders, and very well-spoken. His manners were irreproachable, and when he left, Mrs. Goodwin remarked, "the Atkins are very good customers."

Soon Harlan's visits to the store became frequent. There was always some errand for shaving soap or shoelaces. Lately, when he walked through the door, Mrs. Goodwin greeted him and then excused herself and pretended to be busy in the back room, in order to leave them alone.

VII.

Baseball practice started with playing catch, loosening up while waiting for everyone to arrive. Harlan tossed a ball with Tommy Briggs, while his friend Cornelius threw with another teammate. Harlan had the impression that Cornelius was avoiding him. Why? Cornelius had said little since the night at the Love Tabernacle. As if he was embarrassed.

What was it about joy that people found unsettling? Harlan wondered. Was Cornelius actually *frightened?*

The Morgantown team was a mix of grown men and teenagers, centering on a few players of natural ability, such as the captain, Big Sam Dobbs, a railroad man who knew how to pitch, and Harlan, who was the best shortstop in the county. Some of the older fellows should've quit long ago to make room for new faces, but it was impossible to force them. Morris Meadows, the right-fielder, was 60 years old, painfully slow, and still insisted on playing bare-handed. He scorned gloves as a foolish and unmanly innovation. The second baseman Nathaniel Rhodes, known to everyone as The Gnat, was a problem, too. Barely five feet tall, he'd been spry in his youth but over the years he'd acquired a sagging belly which hung over his belt and impeded his ability to bend over for ground balls. He was a fat Gnat.

"Mind if I join you?"

Reverend Stillhouse, pastor of the Methodist church, stepped up to throw with Harlan and Tommy Briggs. Nothing wrong with a three-way warm-up, of course, but Harlan found the man's presence rather peculiar. The Reverend occasionally umpired or filled in if they were short-handed, but he didn't attend practices. Why had he shown up?

Is he checking up on me? Harlan wondered. Perhaps he'd got wind of the Love Tabernacle. This notion was a trifle annoying but it also amused him. Well, so be it. A Methodist stuffed-shirt could enter the Love Tabernacle, too.

"You missed an interesting sermon last Friday," Harlan said, tossing the ball to Stillhouse.

"That so?" Stillhouse threw to Briggs.

"Yes. The promise of love is everywhere."

As the ball made another round, Stillhouse remarked, "We need to know where to look."

A lingering glance—*yes*, thought Harlan. It's not my imagination. He hasn't come to play. He's here to sniff around.

"Love in action speaks for itself." Harlan threw the ball with an extra zing, and Reverend Stillhouse winced when it smacked his glove. "It's not just a show for Sundays."

"I was gonna go Friday night," interjected Briggs, "but we had trouble at home."

They turned to him.

"Everything all right?" Stillhouse asked.

Briggs beckoned with his glove, inviting another throw, and Stillhouse tossed gently.

After the ball reached him, Briggs announced, "Our best cow, Warts, got struck by lightning."

Harlan and the Reverend expressed their regrets at this misfortune as the ball went round again. Then, after a respectful silence, Harlan flipped his wrist and sent the ball in the other direction, reversing the flow, and he resumed speaking about the Love Tabernacle.

He described Wilbur Wilson and his family. "You know, Reverend, their simplicity is part of the message. I look at those people and think, if Jesus were here today, that's how he'd be living. I believe that. He wouldn't be cooped up. He'd be out spreading the love."

The Reverend caught the ball and held onto it, stopping the activity. He obliged them to wait while he spoke. "Providence is at work in our congregation, too. Love takes many forms, Harlan."

Then he threw.

Harlan wasn't impressed. "I suppose so. But what I experienced Friday was a different kind of power."

Briggs said, "Didn't do Warts no good."

VIII.

That afternoon Fanny went out to the alley behind the store and dipped a pail into the basin below the rain spout. Mrs. Goodwin collected rainwater for its softness, and used it to wash her bottles of tinctures and extract.

Fanny looked down into the pail and saw a face. Her reflection momentarily startled her—she'd performed this task many times without such a glimpse—it was no doubt a question of the angle, the light. Now she paused to look at this young woman who shimmered and faded then came back again. A view of herself from above, like God.

What next? she whispered.

Fanny felt a nervousness such as she'd never known. She had only one life and it was important that she use it well. And the truth was, it vexed her that people thought she should be grateful to Harlan. She was fond of him, but she didn't understand his eager talk, especially lately.

She couldn't shake a sense that when people like Harlan talked about God they could see only one thing, their own reflection, while God, if God was real, got stuck with witnessing everything.

Poor God, thought Fanny.

IX.

From the mound, Big Sam Dobbs threw batting practice. Each Morgantown player took a turn at the plate while the others fielded. The sun climbed high and the day grew hot. Big Sam bore down. Now he threw with full velocity, his shirt untucked, and the batters struggled. Finally Big Sam let his arm fall limp at his side and said he'd had enough.

"Think we can beat the Clowns?"

His teammates cheered. "We'll destroy the Clowns! Destroy the Clowns!"

Big Sam laughed and went behind the backstop, where there was a well. He jacked the pump-handle furiously till water gushed, and then stuck his head under it. Players took turns drinking and slapping the cold water on their necks. Harlan hung back, letting others go first. Cornelius, he noticed, took his turn and left the ballfield without waiting for him.

After dousing his head and drinking his fill, Harlan started to walk home. Soon he came up behind The Gnat, who was limping along the road.

"You all right?"

"Damn blisters. Maybe I should just pop them and be done with it."

Harlan adjusted his pace. "But today was fun, wasn't it? Makes my heart rejoice in creation."

The Gnat stopped and sat in the dirt. Mumbling to himself, he pulled off a shoe. Harlan tried not to stare at The Gnat's big belly, so he focused instead on the bald spot on top of his head, which was sunburned a bright red. The Gnat pressed on a blister with his thumbnail. He let out a yip. He pressed again, another yip. Then he tied on his shoe, panting.

"Better?" said Harlan.

The Gnat snapped, "You want something, kid?"

This reaction surprised Harlan. "Well, no. I don't want any-thing." The Gnat lurched himself upright. "The gift has already been given."

Harlan had never spoken at length with this man. Most en-counters had been at the post office, where The Gnat, as Mor-gantown postmaster, sold him stamps. The Gnat moved away and Harlan wondered what Wilbur Wilson would say in these circumstances. He called, "The gift is yours, too."

The Gnat kept going, so Harlan came up beside him and began to describe the Love Tabernacle. He didn't get far. "I know all about it," The Gnat interrupted. "We're gonna be born again, like Judas."

Harlan smiled. "Actually, that's not how the story goes."

"Oh, it's not? Maybe you're referring to Nicodemus, who came to visit Jesus at night. He got told to get born again."

Harlan nodded. "Yes, that's the one."

"Well, that's not what I'm talking about, you condescending little jackass."

Harlan stopped in his tracks. "What?"

The Gnat stopped, too. He hitched up his pants and curled his lower lip. "How did Judas die?"

"Huh?" Harlan thought for a moment, retrieving what he'd learned at his Methodist Sunday School. "He hung himself. Af-ter he betrayed Jesus."

"Yeah, one part of the New Testament refers to hanging. Read a bit further, and you get a different death. It says that Judas fell headlong and he burst open and his bowels gushed out. Look it up! Now, let me ask you: how can he die twice? Unless Judas was born again."

"You're twisting it around."

"Am I? You're just another one of those cherry-pickers. I betcha I've read that book more closely than you have, kid. So listen, this is the story: it's always the same old thing for humanity, over and over. You might think you're special, Buster, but you're not. Go ahead, get born again. You're going to die again, anyway."

The Gnat limped away.

"Wait a second!"

"Shut up and read your Bible."

X.

"It's not like I was attacking him," Harlan told Fanny. Instead of meeting in the alley, today they'd picked raspberries along the road leading out of town and now sat on a bench under a catalpa tree. "But he didn't want to listen. Nathaniel Rhodes must be an unhappy man."

"We can't know his story."

Insects hummed, and grasshoppers jumped in the weeds of the ditch. Harlan reached up to a low-hanging branch and tore off a large catalpa leaf. He handed it to her so she could use it as a fan. The air was humid and still.

"It's frustrating," he said. "Why do people think so *small?* Like this baseball game, for instance. I've been practicing as hard as anybody but if you consider it for five seconds, it serves no purpose. Why bother? It doesn't really mean anything."

"Does it have to?" Fanny agitated the leaf. "Aren't you tak-ing this too seriously? Just the other night you saw the hand of God everywhere. So if it comes to that, why not in baseball?"

Harlan frowned. "I'm seeing so many other things now. It's *people*, Fanny. They're the challenge. Even the Reverend Still-house! I have this bad feeling like something precious is slipping away." His arm slid over her shoulder, but it was too hot for that and she shrugged him off. She reached down to a knotted kerchief on the bench and selected a raspberry. She bit into it, her teeth working on the tiny seeds.

"So what are people supposed to do?"

"We can't settle for something small, Fanny. Let's talk about our plans."

She sat up straighter. That tone of voice again, trying to convince her. Harlan had already spoken of getting formally en-gaged when he reached his last year at the university; they could marry after his graduation when he came back to Morgantown and settled down. Fanny was flattered by these speculations but they left her wondering. All that was years from now. Easy for Harlan to say. His ardor carried him away.

"What if I didn't go to the university?" he asked. "What if we got married right away? We could leave this place and see the world. The entire Love Tabernacle is spread out before us. We could share it with each other, and with all the interesting people we encounter along the way."

She stopped fanning herself.

"Not go to the university? Are you serious?"

"Yes! Why not? That's a useless delay. Honestly, what are we waiting for?"

Fanny could see that he meant his words. But this possibility had never occurred to her. Earlier, when he'd spoken of leav-ing Morgantown for his education, she hadn't questioned the premise. Given the chance, she'd do the same. She envied Harlan in this respect. It went without saying that she could never go to college. College was for other people, people with money: college was an inside joke. Anyone on the outside knew this. In the fall Harlan would say goodbye to this place, while she would stay with Mrs. Goodwin and read her wall of books. Any plans beyond those were impossible to predict.

"What about your parents?" she asked. "I don't think they would be too pleased with this idea."

"Oh, they'll get over it. Frankly, they lack imagination. But they'll learn. Besides, the question isn't them. It's us." He took her hand. "Fanny, we could go to Africa!"

She blinked. She was confused. "What? Africa?" Now he squeezed her hand, leaning in, and she tried to joke, her voice coming out scratchy: "*Africa?* In a wagon?"

He jumped up and began to pace.

"You don't see, do you? You really don't see? It's not because of your folks at home, is it?"

They'd generally avoided the subject of her family, and now this allusion seemed ill-timed. Was he talking down to her? Implying that *she* was being limited? She pictured her brothers, seeding clover and butchering hogs; her father, worrying over crops. The perseverance of their lives.

"Harlan," she said, "you're talking like a little boy."

He froze.

"That's how Nathaniel Rhodes spoke to me. Is that what you really think? I would've never put you two on the same page."

"I speak only for myself."

"But look at you!" he said. "I can't believe it. You're already resigned. You don't want the Tabernacle? You'd settle for being another Judas?"

"Judas?" she said. "What on earth? My goodness!"

Now Fanny was angry. Harlan began to explain about The Gnat and dying a second time but she could make no sense of it.

"I don't care about him!" she said. "This has nothing to do with him. But I do know this much, Harlan. You don't get to talk to me that way. No one does!"

Fanny rose from the bench.

"Wait!"

"I can find my own way home."

XI.

On the day of the game against the Mungo Clowns, Harlan stayed in his bedroom and refused to come downstairs. The Doctor and Eunice Atkins called up to him, but to no avail. A message went out. This was a very awkward development.

Big Sam Dobbs arrived at the house on a bicycle and was admitted into Harlan's bedroom where he attempted to change his mind, but Dobbs left without success. Morgantown would have to find another shortstop.

"Won't you at least come down for a cup of coffee?" his mother called. "I've got plum cake."

"I'm studying!" he shouted.

The Doctor and his wife looked at each other.

"What do we do?" she asked. "It makes me nervous. He's so quiet."

The Doctor was irritated at this juvenile display. "We're not going to humor him. We're stepping out."

"Out? Where?"

"To the baseball game, of course! He'll see us from his window and will know where we're going. He'll see how ridiculously he's behaving."

He selected a hat while Eunice prepared a jar of lemonade. They left via the front porch and headed down the street.

"There's a silver lining in all this," the Doctor said, pressing his lips together.

"What's that?"

"We're rid of that shop girl."

Up in his bedroom, Harlan bent over his Bible. He wanted to dig his way out of this mess, out of this darkness, and to do that, he needed to retreat. If people would just leave him alone, maybe he could sort it out.

But it was hard to focus. It was hard to make sense.

Why had the Love Tabernacle moved on without him? That was how he felt, as if he'd been granted a vision only to have it snatched away by the pettiness of others. He was bereft. Why couldn't he recapture that insight? He looked up from his Bible, rubbing the side of his face. Was this a test?

What he'd experienced had been real, he would swear with all the force of his being. But a veil had fallen over the luster of life. Why? Why? And now he was supposed to settle for *baseball?*

He brought his palms together and closed his eyes and tried to pray. *Bring me back what I have seen. Oh please.* But his mind faltered. He felt he was tumbling forward into a different kind of existence.

Harlan opened his eyes and turned up his right palm. He wanted to speak to Fanny. He imagined her face. "I do love you, you know." Oh, look at her. Those serious eyes, that mouth. She was beautiful. A breeze moved a wisp of hair on her forehead. Wait—was there someone next to her? Yes, it was Mrs. Goodwin from the store. But they weren't at the store, there was a crowd—more people—was that Reverend Stillhouse, too? Harlan turned up his left palm and brought his hands together, and spread before him he saw his parents, with other spectators, his old high school teachers and Johnny Wales talking to Catfish who patted the head of a flop-eared dog, and on the field, The Gnat at second base and Big Sam pitching and look, Cornelius had replaced him at shortstop! The Mungo Clowns stood along the third base line, cheering on their batter, a tall man in an absurd green top hat, while out in right field, old Morris Meadows watched in wonder as a spot of earth trembled in front of his feet. The soil crumbled. The ground opened. Emerging from below into the light, a mole crawled out shakily, bleeding, and then before his eyes, the creature expired. Harlan looked down at them all in his cupped hands, and his heart ached.

THREE

Paris, 1925

Gertie and the Babe

Perhaps it was inevitable, but the identity switch between Gertrude Stein and Babe Ruth in the winter of 1925 has now been confirmed by Professor Lucille Cauvet of the University of Paris-Nanterre following the discovery of a lost cache of telegrams. With this material proof in hand, along with the testimony of diaries and transatlantic ship logs, Professor Cauvet has now set the record straight.

It all started one December morning in Paris when a tiny woman recognized the baseball star strolling down the boulevard Raspail. She introduced herself as Alice, admitted that she'd always rooted for the Giants, but said it would be an honor if an esteemed American like Mr. Ruth came to lunch.

Her nervous, birdlike face startled him, but her timing was perfect. The Babe had grown weary of his holiday, and found it a relief to speak English and to be understood. A home-cooked meal—why not?

So he followed her home and planted himself before the table and, after the second bottle of wine had been poured, he began to open up, to tell Alice and another woman present, a stocky, square lady with a big voice, about how he'd turned down the opportunity to go on a barnstorming tour in the Far East in order to take some time in the off-season to think over his future.

"You play the game of baseball, do I understand correctly, Mr. Ruth?"

Alice put in quickly, "Gertrude cares only about writing, about literature. We miss out on a lot of things living here."

The Babe laughed. "No worries, kid." He looked around the room. "So it wasn't you who painted all these pictures?"

The ladies laughed, and he realized that he'd said something foolish, but he didn't mind, because it relieved him of the obligation of thinking up a compliment for this queer-looking art. People got up to all kinds of things nowadays. He and Gertrude tucked in and finished the platter of chicken and the conversation shifted to the Yankees. Alice asked him about his injuries, about the famous belly-ache that had sidelined him that summer. He avoided the truth (he wasn't going to talk to these ladies about his venereal problems!) and repeated a story about having consumed too many hot dogs.

"Yes, that's what I read in the papers," said Alice. "You must be very fond of frankfurters."

The Babe shrugged. "A hot dog is a hot dog is a hot dog."

Gertrude looked on with an absorbed expression and he could tell that she was taking in his every word. It wasn't often that a non-fan showed such interest, and over the third bottle of wine, the Babe began to unburden his heart. He felt liberated and safe in the company of strangers. For the first time he admitted aloud what a disappointment the 1925 season had been, when he'd slumped below a .300 batting average and the Yankees had floundered to seventh place, an astonishing 28 and ½ games behind the pennant-winning Washington Senators.

"You can turn the page," Alice reassured. "You can find the old form, Mr. Ruth. People will forget about 1925 Senators. They will remember *your* achievements."

"Will they?" he asked.

For months the Babe had been nagged by doubts, losing faith in his gifts. Was he washed up?

Now Gertrude sat up straight, wiped her mouth with her napkin and declared, "You, sir, are bellyaching too much. It's only a game. How hard can it be?"

The Babe couldn't believe his ears. This Alice was a nice gal but this other one—*huh?* Never had anyone spoken to him this way!

"Listen, lady, what do you know?"

"I know very much, as a matter of fact. Take my advice, and your talent will do the rest. You have seen the thing, Mr. Ruth, which is the thing you have seen, and having seen the thing that you have seen, you must to continue to see it. This is so."

"You write stuff?" He tossed down the rest of his glass. "That's what you do?"

"And she gives opinions," said Alice. "She tells people what to do."

"I see," he muttered. "How hard could *that* be?"

"I don't think you'd like to try it, sir."

✿

Often geniuses arrive at the same idea simultaneously, but it is rare that it happens to geniuses in such widely different fields. And perhaps it was possible because of their mutual skepticism. Probably the experiment would never have taken place if not for Alice, the go-between, the facilitator.

The first part was easy, and it still didn't seem quite serious when Gertrude put on the Babe's serge suit and raccoon coat and accepted his passport. From his side, the transition required less effort, because Gertrude's silk kimonos suited him more comfortably than game-day pinstripes, especially in light of the effects of Alice's cooking, and the Bambino's growing girth. "I could get used to this!" he chuckled, putting his feet up and leaning back on a rattan settee.

Gertrude struggled in April and May, striking out three times in a game against Boston and once, in Cleveland, misplaying a routine fly ball so badly that fans and sportswriters were scratching their heads. But she was tenacious, made adjustments, and her batting average steadily improved, while her power was never in question. (Gertrude was a naturally lofty swinger.) By July, she was hitting over .300 and made one of the most memorable plays of the season when she caught a sacrifice fly in deep right field and threw out Ty Cobb sliding headfirst into home plate. A double play! On her way back to the dugout, the inning over, she trotted past Cobb who was still arguing with the umpire and she haughtily tipped her cap at the irate Tiger. The crowd roared with delight, and Cobb's reaction—livid, obscene, rolling on the ground as the umpire grappled to restrain him—led to his month-long suspension.

Meanwhile, back in Paris, Ruth's earlier pleasures began to pale. All sorts of people came round to rue de Fleurus and he quickly grew tired of them. The telegrams he exchanged with Stein at this time are revealing. Upon receiving Stein's lapidary message, *"Lefty Grove—what?"*, he sent this troubled reply:

"Make him pitch you inside. GERTIE, who ARE all these weirdos? What am I supposed to SAY to them? G Leblanc—neurasthenia—what? I WON'T do NUDE for Picasso! Hemingway—freeloader— needs title—what? This joint is a madhouse!"

Clearly, the Babe didn't like the situation and was groping to find his way. Similar telegrams streamed in almost daily from Paris, while Gertrude's replies were sporadic and sometimes cryptic, leaving much to interpretation. For instance, her July 28 message:

"Cadence—Cadence—your only Fiesta!"

Frankly, the Babe was getting fed up, and Alice had to fetch him home one night when he sneaked away to spend the evening in the company of some rue Blondel floozies and returned, much the worse for drink, to evict the hangers-on at Gertrude's place with shouts and fisticuffs. "OUT of here! You can all get LOST and stay LOST! YOU CAN QUOTE ME ON THAT!"

Young Ernest trudged off into the darkness, snuffling.

It was an unhappy evening but it seemed to clear the air a bit. Alice consoled him in following days with a leg of lamb with broad beans and a large serving of her special brownies, after which his edges of vision throbbed warmly and the art on the walls acquired a new significance. Back in New York, Gertrude had managed to lift the Yankees to the top of the American League, a remarkable achievement which included 12 of her 46 homers hit to the opposite field (look it up!) which, though undeniably impressive, was not enough to carry them through the World Series against St. Louis, which the Yankees lost when Gertrude rashly tried to steal second base in the ninth inning of the seventh game. It was an embarrassing exit, and received more publicity than it deserved, because of course the club wouldn't have reached such heights without her earlier, and enormous, contributions. Still, it revealed, incontestably, a state of fatigue. It had been a long season. Her October 10 telegram announced: "*Time to come home.*"

The Babe was in full agreement. Yes, it was time.

Thus the experiment ended. Upon her arrival at the rue de Fleurus, Gertrude hugged Alice so hard that she aggravated Alice's scoliosis, and put her in the Hôpital Lariboisière for three days. The Babe, though he would miss Alice's grub, was eager to return to his true calling and seems to have recovered his focus and motivation, in his mighty efforts to surpass the impressive stats that Gertrude had racked up in 1926. Would Ruth have managed his amazing 1927 season, with 60 home runs, if not for his Parisian hiatus? In a forthcoming article in the *Revue française d'études américaines,* Professor Cauvet explores such questions. Would Stein have attempted her subsequent forays into operatic libretti, if not for the remembered polyphony of bleachers in the Bronx? They needed each other without knowing it. Such is history—such is humanity.

FOUR

Raccoon River Valley, 1937

Heaven

At first they were delighted when the Enochville Swallows came from behind and won the game. The team had struggled all season. It felt good to cheer. A decisive victory on the following day was even more surprising.

They finished the season by winning their last eleven outings. This unexpected streak kept everyone talking all winter, speculating about future prospects. Photos of ballplayers suddenly appeared on the walls in bars and diners.

The following April, Mayor Portis threw out the first pitch and the Swallows won again! After four straight victories, demand for tickets soared and there weren't enough seats to accommodate the newly-minted fans. That was when the mayor lobbied successfully for eminent domain and the destruction of a nearby ciderworks, which a wrecking ball reduced to dust. New earth was turned. An additional grandstand beyond the outfield ensured that everyone could enjoy the action.

How did Jerry Mercer make that incredible flying catch in the ninth? What accounted for Dolph Camelli's uncanny curve ball in his two consecutive perfect games? Who could explain Bobby Sheets, the light-hitting second baseman, stepping up to the plate and jacking a tie-breaking home run that sailed over the astonished faces in the new grandstand before landing in Walter Baum's vegetable garden and bouncing over his hedge and splashing in Rose Kindley's bird bath? The ball was brought back to Billy for an autograph and charitably auctioned off at a price to pay the city's operational budget for schools, police, and fire department. Mayor Portis held a press conference and announced, "We shall abolish all taxes."

On the Fourth of July, the Swallows were still undefeated, the longest winning streak ever. Families put out blankets on the grass to watch the fireworks show, recalling with incredulous laughter the previous season when Dolph Camelli had blown a game by walking in a batter with the bases loaded, or when the team had squandered a six-run lead and Bobby Sheets took a called third strike for the final out, whereupon he ducked his eyes amid the boos and slouched dejectedly off the diamond. A few people, though, claimed that he'd ripped off his helmet in disgust and dashed it to the ground, frustrated tears visible on his face. People took pleasure in disputing different versions of that humiliation.

But this season offered no such denials: it was unstinting victory, game after game. One night near the end of July, the Swallows fell behind by nine runs in the first three innings, and it appeared the streak would end. Spectators leaned in closer, their throats going dry. The air was sticky, expectant, still.

Then gale winds descended upon Enochville, a thunderstorm with torrents of rain. Lightning struck the scoreboard and the roof of the concession stand got blown off. The game was a wash-out.

The next day, skies were blue, the air scrubbed pure. Wise folks who'd saved their rain checks redeemed them that afternoon at a make-up contest where, starting afresh, the Swallows won. That evening they also prevailed in the regularly-scheduled game, thus sweeping the double-header.

By August, it was easy to spot empty rows in the grandstands. Ticket prices dropped, though the team's record was still unblemished. People avoided the turnstiles and sought other distractions. In Enochville's bars a new fashion emerged for betting on blindfold billiards, and in diners conversations turned away from the games to discuss philately and dialectical materialism. Everywhere in town, business fell off as patrons drifted away.

When school resumed in September, local teachers succumbed to pressure from Mayor Portis to organize field trips to the ballpark to watch the undefeated Swallows, whose example offered pupils lessons about life and success. These outings also helped to fill the empty seats. Kids grumbled that the games lasted an eternity, but no one paid attention to their harping. People were sick of baseball.

FIVE

Sogo Ground Baseball Park, 1950

Little Boy and the Carp

Why did she come to see the Carp? Perhaps to look inside the newly-constructed stadium, or to glimpse the young men in their red-lettered uniforms. Taking pre-game infield practice, they scooped up ground balls, while along the first-base line, a lean young pitcher warmed up with a whipping sidearm, and in the outfield, teammates played long-distance catch in high looping arcs. Everything moved at a different speed but it also seemed part of a harmonious process, like a sewing machine with crank and hook and bobbin, stitching together a pattern. She wasn't fond of baseball. The final form of this pattern had yet to emerge. Still, she felt irresistibly drawn here, like a witness for others who were absent.

"I'm as good as he is."

"Hah! Maybe half as fast."

Teenage boys in the row ahead of her discussed the Carp's pitcher, who kicked his leg and let fly.

"I'm serious. Next year, that could be me out there!"

"You're dreaming."

An older man in the same row leaned in. "Next year?" He laughed. "You might be dead."

He had a scorched face and she suspected that he'd been drinking. Uneasily the boys laughed along with him. For an instant the action on the field disappeared. Everything moved inside and they were thinking the same thing. It didn't matter that they were strangers. She could remember if she chose, but she didn't like to share it.

✱

Five years ago, her son had pestered her first thing in the morning, demanding an early breakfast. The day was already hot. Other children would claim the field where he was eager to play. "I need to go now. They're waiting for me."

"No they're not. Sit down and eat."

He'd started to do his *bird-hop*. That was the term his father had coined before he'd gone away to join his regiment. When the boy was excited he couldn't keep still and he talked animatedly, fluttering his hands and sometimes his feet actually left the ground. He was like a little bird on the cusp of flight who would take off immediately if he weren't in this cage. These days were hard on children, being cooped up. Now her son swung an imaginary baseball bat, hopping.

"I can't miss it."

"You heard me," she said. "Sit down."

He ate quickly. She watched him with a mix of irritation and amusement. She'd slept badly last night, lonely in her room. After he finished his breakfast, she still made him wait. When the siren sounded, she told him he could go.

"You will be good!" she called.

"I'll be good!"

He didn't look back. Other children poured into the street; her son was greeted by a boy with a pointy face and his hair parted down the middle, the son of a glass-cutter, and they ran off together. She yawned and closed the door and went to her place next to the window where she'd set up her sewing machine to take advantage of the light. She heard the creaking of a pushcart and the high-pitched squeals of little girls as they trotted by.

✸

When the game started, the teenage boys lit up cigarettes and, as an afterthought, offered one to the older man who happily accepted, biting down on the end, showing his teeth in his little round hole of a mouth. She disapproved of them but she couldn't say why. Perhaps it was a quality of their voices, frivolous voices, more perceptible as feeling than as actual conversation. She wanted to ignore them in the same way she tried to ignore the persistent aches in her joints, because she also felt a love coursing through her as she watched a player lope across the field with easy grace. It was like a memory of something she'd never seen.

The grass was resplendent green. The sky blue and empty. There was a silence if you listened for it. She imagined thousands of shadows walking around the city and filling the electric trams and boats on the river.

"Oh no!"

An opponent drilled a long fly ball that landed between two Carp outfielders and rolled up to the fence. A player on base ahead of him raced around toward home.

"Wait! Wait!"

But the throw was late: the runner slid across the plate.

The teenage boys slapped their knees.

"It can't be helped," said the older man.

In the excitement, she'd risen to her feet and added her own voice to the shouting crowd. Her heart beat faster; she felt the capillaries pulsing in her neck, a band of heat up her spine. Presently the action slowed again, and a breeze parted the air.

❖

The bomb, she'd learned later, was called Little Boy. That was what they said. The Americans had pushed Little Boy out of an airplane.

She was working at the window, sewing a collar for her husband's great-aunt, a wily old woman who'd stopped by on the pretext of inquiring about her great-nephew. How was he? Any news from the regiment? *No—no news.* Auntie had brought along a bag of mending that she expected would be done free of charge. She helped herself to a palmful of peanuts and announced, "I can come back tomorrow."

"I'm sure you can."

That morning, when she opened the bag, her annoyance softened when she inspected the contents. The faded collar and undersash, the intimate garments that likely dated back to the previous century. She giggled, arranging them in a pile. "Oh, Auntie. Look at you." She went to work. After a few minutes she straightened her back and rested her eyes, a smell of her neighbor's cooking drifting through the window. She thought of her son, his hunger to play, come what may. Her elbow knocked a spool off the edge of the table, and she bent to retrieve it as it rolled away in a half-circle and then returned toward her feet.

Then came a flash—there was no noise—and it seemed the sun was in the room. She didn't know what happened. The light made everything disappear.

SIX

Marion County, 1967

Antennae

On the front porch, a green davenport stood next to an old washing machine with a radio in it. After Sunday dinner Uncle Pearly liked to come out and sit on the davenport, remove the radio and plug it in. He twiddled the radio's big dial, which picked up ballgames in St. Louis.

"Why do you keep the radio in the washing machine?" Tim had asked.

"Sometimes when it rains it blows up against the house." Uncle Pearly leaned back and put his feet up on a fruit crate. "You gotta think ahead in life."

This was the third Sunday in a row that Tim and his mother had visited their country relatives. Church and a chicken dinner, and he wondered at this new routine. Before, they'd stayed in town and he'd played baseball with Daddy. They had their own version of the game. Daddy lay in bed, and Tim bounced a rubber ball against the side of the house. He fielded grounders or caught a carom in the air. In the beginning his mother had told him not to create a disturbance but Daddy protested that he liked the sound of Tim playing. So then his mother encouraged him. The game had imaginary adversaries and followed rules of his own invention, rules that emerged from his head like a tune that he improvised by whistling. Once he'd spied Daddy's pale thin face in the window, watching. It was as if the bed wouldn't hold Daddy.

Now, on Sundays at the farm, his mother and Aunt Edie invited him to play with his cousin Dean. But where to begin? Dean was a two-and-a half year old toddler and he hadn't mastered his toilet training. Last week, when Tim handed him a ball, Dean bugged out his eyes and took a prodigious dump in his pants.

"Oh, don't worry!" said Aunt Edie, rushing over. "That happens sometimes."

She tried to play it down, but, later in the day, when Tim attempted to sing a song for his cousin, Dean bugged out his eyes and did it again. Since then, Tim had kept a careful distance, not wanting to set him off.

❁

Where was heaven? Tim had recently pondered this question and now, at the dinner table, it occupied him anew. Heaven wasn't a place in outer space, not exactly. Because if you had a map of the universe you could point to planets and constellations but heaven was somewhere else, not on the map. A mystery of creation.

"It's hot as hell," complained Uncle Pearly, sucking on a bone.

Tim's father had never used such language but it was indeed the warmest Sunday yet, unrelentingly humid. It had been a mercy to get out of their church clothes but everyone was still sweating and there was nothing you could do about it. Uncle Pearly reached for the gravyboat and doused his potatoes. He had pink cheeks and a bald head like a speckled egg.

"Tim, you can have the other drumstick," his mother encouraged.

"Thanks." He served himself from the platter, aware of others' eyes. Everyone was trying to be nice to him. It wasn't only what they said and did, but also the way they looked at him. This last part he didn't like, and he wished he could be invisible.

"Gaaah," said cousin Dean, banging his spoon.

After dessert Tim excused himself and went to the front screen door, opening it very slowly, pulling it all the way back. The door was on a tight spring. On the porch, cats had gathered and sprawled snoozing on the davenport. They came up from the barn and it was their favorite place to congregate when people were away. Everything was still. Tim whispered, *"Let there be cats."*

He released his grip and the door slammed violently.

An explosion of cats! Startled, they leaped in all directions, off the side of the porch or straight up into the air and over the rail into the bushes.

Tim found this reaction very satisfying. But it was a fleeting pleasure, and when he opened the door again and let himself out onto the porch, the rest of the afternoon stretched before him.

These Sundays were endless. Adult voices reached him from inside the house but he willed himself not to make out their meaning. Tim headed down the steps, in search of relief.

✻

Under a mulberry tree behind the house Uncle Pearly had parked an old Rambler station wagon. It had been there for as long as Tim could remember, and there was something unearthly about it. Stripped of its tires, the car perched on cinder blocks and looked as if it had been left behind by a high tide.

Last Sunday, Tim had slipped into the front seat and got behind the steering wheel and pretended to pilot a rocket ship. He'd blasted himself away from this place.

But today it was too hot to sit in the car. Instead, he climbed up the rear bumper and onto the roof of the Rambler, where he had an easy reach of mulberries.

The fruit was delicious. Tim picked berries quickly, stuffing them in his mouth, his fingers and lips staining blue as if bruised. He looked out beyond the back yard, to the gravel road and lumpy purple clouds on the horizon.

Wherever it was, heaven was far away.

When he had his fill of berries he jumped down from the roof and proceeded around the side of the house, where he saw a grasshopper pop up, dissolve into light and disappear. Where did it go?

Sometimes he believed that he could see things that weren't there. Or he could hear things in forbidden spaces, like when Daddy had pressed his teeth together and turned his face to the wall. Daddy was usually quiet but at times like these he was even quieter—the sort of quiet Tim could hear.

Now a voice startled him.

"I really wish, Tim, that you would not slam the door."

His mother spoke through the kitchen screen window where she stood at the sink, washing dishes. He had stepped into a space where she could observe him. Her voice was full of forced patience. She wanted to scold him, he could tell.

"Sorry," he called up into the air and moved out of sight as quickly as he could.

❖

"Over here, buddy. Got a piece of advice."

Back around the front of the house, Uncle Pearly was setting up his radio on the porch. Tim went as far as the bottom step. "What?"

"Never run through a screen door," his uncle said. "You might strain yourself."

A gnat buzzed by Tim's ear. He slapped it.

His uncle adjusted the dial, searching a clear signal. "Awful lot of static in the air today."

He tilted his head, listening.

"*A ground ball to second . . . Javier scoops it up. One out.*"

Uncle Pearly smiled and sat down on the davenport.

"Shoo."

A striped cat slinked off.

But the static returned, so Uncle Pearly got up and went back to the radio. When he touched the dial, the sound became clear again. He frowned, removing his hand. More static. "Come up here, will ya?" Tim climbed the steps and joined his uncle. "Just put your hand on top. Right there." Tim obeyed. "*Strike two!*" Uncle Pearly smiled and returned to the davenport.

Touching the warm radio, hearing the crowd roar, Tim was transported from the farm and he saw a distant city and a tall stadium that buzzed like a giant beehive. Inside, tens of thousands of people looked down as a mighty contest played out on the diamond. Above, the sky was an open vault.

"Try lifting your other arm," Uncle Pearly suggested.

Tim obeyed.

"*A line drive straight up the middle! Here comes the runner. And the throw—*"

It was an exciting game. St. Louis scored two runs and took the lead.

"Move your arm this way. Right—that's better."

Tim rested between innings, during the commercial breaks. Uncle Pearly scratched his knees and analyzed the action. "It all depends on whether they'll need to make a pitching change."

"How long is this gonna last?"

"Can't say. We don't get to make the rules."

Tim alternated arms, which made the task easier, though he wondered how long he could go on, stuck where he was. He recalled a Saturday movie matinee he'd attended with his parents about a year ago, a feature called *The Frozen Boy*, which was the story of a prehistoric youth in a leopardskin toga who was found trapped in a block of ice, with a club in his hand, who was put on exhibition by a scientist. People came from far away to marvel at The Frozen Boy, till one day there was a refrigeration problem, the ice melted and the youth ran wild in a screaming crowd, though eventually he was captured, calmed, learned to talk, and by the end of the film he'd cut his hair and put on a suit and married the scientist's daughter.

Tim's father was fine then. That day in the theater they'd sucked on hot cinnamon rock candies and enjoyed the show together. Tim could still remember the taste on his tongue. But time had kept moving, it wasn't frozen, and then came the day when his mother had sent him outside to play ball against the wall. It was sunny and the birds were chorusing. A car pulled up to the house and the doctor jumped out with his bag and hurried up the sidewalk. Tim tried to play, but he stopped often to look up at the window. No one was there.

Then came his mother's voice, thinner than he'd ever heard it:

"You can come in now."

He would never forget that voice. Never. Because he knew. He didn't have to go inside.

He knew. He dropped to his knees and the ball rolled away.

✿

"And the great thing about the farm is you're free," Uncle Pearly was saying, "no neighbors breathing down your neck, it's all yours—" He passed his hand through the air in a gesture that encompassed the front yard, the ditch and weeds, the oceans of pasture beyond the porch. "You do whatever you want!"

The seventh inning had just finished, Tim rubbed his bicep while the radio crackled and his uncle held forth.

"Now we used to have the Cole family living down the road, about two miles south? They were a bad bunch. Used to be, the Cole boys would attend ballgames in town in order to spy on who was present, and if they saw a neighbor, they'd slip away in the middle innings and go and steal their chickens."

Uncle Pearly leaned sideways on the davenport, squinched his eyes and farted. "Catch it and paint it yellow," he said. When Tim didn't react, he continued:

"Fortunately the Cole boys moved out and now a dumb Dutchman lives there but he don't mean no harm. You get a bit older, buddy, I'll let you use my Remington twenty-two. A fellow can do a lot with a squirrel gun."

Tim sensed that his uncle was trying to be friendly in a different manner than he would've done in the presence of his mother and Aunt Edie. He was acting manly. Tim wasn't sure if he liked it.

"And Dean?" said Uncle Pearly. "Oh, he's a pistol! You'll get to know him like a brother."

Tim studied his uncle's face, replaying his words in his head and suddenly, he saw something far beyond. Oh, it couldn't be!

No! But he remembered other hints and inflections, and the cold hard fact that his mother had brought over a wicker chair last Sunday and it was now in the front room of the farmhouse. He'd assumed that she was lending it to Aunt Edie. And today she'd brought canning jars and quilts.

Was it true?

He asked, "We're not gonna come live here, are we?"

Uncle Pearly was slow to answer. "You'll have to talk to your Mom about that."

Something moved in Tim's gut. He left the radio and pounded down the porch steps while Uncle Pearly called after him, "Come back! Game's not over yet!"

Where? Where could he flee?

The Dutchman down the road, if he went that way, couldn't help him. If he ran in the other direction, it was six miles to reach town. That was too far. Tim circled behind the house, to the fence line where white feathers from Aunt Edie's plucked chickens lay strewn on the ground. She threw the guts over the fence and the cats fought like fiends over them.

He felt trapped. The air was muggier now, and strangely still; his shirt clung to his skin. He ran over to the Rambler station wagon, pulled open the door and jumped in. He slammed the door shut.

Curling his fingers into fists, he struck the dashboard. "Hell!" That was a bad word and he wasn't supposed to say it but he repeated, "Hell hell hell." He rocked in the seat, sweat beading on his face. The atmosphere was stifling and smelled of mildew and he tried to roll down his window, but it was stuck.

Where? Where?

He rested his head against the steering wheel, breathing hard. When he looked up again, he noticed movement in the world outside. Dead leaves skipped and skittered along the ground and past the dirty windshield. It was as if the Rambler was hurtling forward while going nowhere. A wind must've come up, but he couldn't feel it. The car was an airless box. Tim's shirt was soaked, even his underwear was growing wet. With a grunt he threw open the door.

He stepped out into the hot wind and climbed up the rear bumper and onto the roof of the car where he unstuck his wet shirt and bared his stomach to the air. He considered taking off his pants, too. The sky looked like it was going to rain but it offered no relief: there were only a few drops. The clouds were not only purple but green, too. Churning. He gazed up into the mulberry tree and imagined himself climbing higher and higher. At the top he would flap his arms and fly away.

"*Tim! Tim!*"

At the sound of his mother's voice, he grabbed onto a branch and swung himself up into the trembling leaves. She wouldn't find him here. He contemplated the next branch and felt the wind growing stronger, like a gust of exhalation from above. Dry twigs and berries broke away and flew off. A broken spider web waved ragged filaments. Suddenly, the tree trunk groaned, a cry of life, straining, twisting against the years of rings inside.

"*Tim! Tim!*"

There was distress in her voice. And for the first time, Tim felt afraid. Not for himself, but for his mother. Oh, she'd already had too much trouble. He couldn't leave her behind.

He shifted on his branch and dropped down to the roof of the station wagon, then jumped to the ground. He hastened around the house.

They were all on the porch, waiting as if on a ship deck. His mother, her hair blowing across her cheek. Aunt Edie with Dean on her hip. Uncle Pearly, his pants flapping in the hot air. Tim ran up the steps to join them. "Here I am! Here I am!" She grasped his shoulders and he put his arms around her waist.

Then came the hail. Tim heard it first, crashing against the house, before he turned to see it bouncing in the grass, round, the color of spit. The ice seemed alive, speckling the green. A cat streaked across the yard, followed by another cat, zagging in a different direction, exposed. Cousin Dean began to wail.

"Let's get inside!" shouted Aunt Edie.

Uncle Pearly grappled with his cord and disconnected the radio, and Tim's mother pulled him toward the screen door. But he broke free when he saw a man walking in the front yard, ice falling all around him.

Could they see him?

Could they see Daddy?

Look! Look at him curl his lips. He showed his teeth, and his chest all of a sudden pushed out, like his own self was more than he could contain. Daddy moved slowly but calmly around the corner of the house, on his way to get behind the wheel of the Rambler.

"Come on," his mother called. She held open the screen door. Aunt Edie and Dean hurried past her, Uncle Pearly secured the radio in the washing machine and followed them, and with a moan Tim put down his head and joined them inside.

SEVEN

Chicago, 1979

Foul

At the ballpark the world began to shimmer strangely. Billy put it down to the previous night at the Big Q and the after-effects of his conversation with Glitter Boy. He shouldn't have listened to that guy. Or even let him in the office. Now, the sun was too bright. The grass looked sinister.

"I love day games," Bonnie said. "Don't you?"

Billy had forgotten his sunglasses. Bonnie wore an oversized pair with hot pink frames. Billy didn't follow baseball or remember the players' names, but it was necessary to keep up appearances now that famous athletes came to the Big Q and left him complementary tickets. They were high-value customers. Maybe he would appear on television when the camera panned across the box seats in search of celebrities and politicians. The lens might linger on Bonnie, who wore a snug T-shirt. Look: that squinting moonfaced man next to the pretty girl must be someone important!

"Were you at the upstairs party last night?" he asked.

"What do you mean? I was working in front at the bar."

"Oh, I forgot. Good."

An organ heaved and they stood for the National Anthem, facing a flag on a distant pole. His father had always told him never to drink on the job or screw around with employees. Since his father's death two years ago, Billy had taken down the Big Q's neon shamrock and removed the pool tables; he'd put in a

dance floor and a mirror ball. He'd remodeled his father's upstairs office, where he spent a lot of time drinking on the job
and hosting private parties with waitresses. Business was booming. "*And the home—of the—brave!*"

"I'm always downstairs," Bonnie added when they sat down,
as if to make sure he wouldn't confuse her with someone else.

An unwanted sensation returned, like a tiny sewing machine
going very fast inside his head. Or maybe it was tiny teeth, gnawing. His skull contained a rodent. He could hear it. *Something*
was going on in there. Last night, Billy had been very drunk
and had confessed this uncomfortable experience to Glitter Boy,
wondering aloud if it could be a tumor or something?

Until recently, Glitter Boy had sold drugs at his club, which
Billy scrupulously pretended not to know about, in order to protect himself—someone was going to do it, so why not Glitter
Boy, who was sly and vicious enough to keep out competitors
and didn't make it Billy's problem. Glitter Boy's customers spent
a lot of money at the Big Q. But lately he'd turned a new leaf; he
spoke of loving Jesus and last night he'd come upstairs to Billy's
office away from the flashing lights and loud music to share his
joy. His eyes looked different—happy, wide open. Eager. In a
previous conversation he'd spoken of using Billy's hot tub for
baptisms. Now he said, "It might not be a tumor. Let me touch
your head."

"Touch my head?"

"The Holy Spirit gives believers the power to cast out
demons." He came around the desk, his hands outstretched. "Let
me try."

"Don't you touch my head!"

Some things were nobody's damn business, the personal
things, the ones you were unsure of yourself. The mysteries.
Billy's father, for instance. Mack Quinn had died on June 4,

which was also Billy's birthday, and in the two years since that grim morning, Billy had often relived the memory of slumping in a chair next to his father's hospital bed when suddenly his father called out, "*Comet!*"

Or something like that. Billy had been on vigil all night and now he snapped awake, leaned closer. "What is it, Dad?" For several days Mack had drifted in and out of consciousness, and the drugs made him slur and talk loopy. Maybe he'd said "Come here!" Or even "Connie!" (Billy's mother, who'd fled Chicago years ago and married a Chrysler dealer in Kenosha.) "Dad?" He grasped the old man's hot hand. "I'm here."

"I don't . . ." Twenty, thirty seconds passed, and Billy had the impression that he was spent, and would say no more. Then, distinctly: "I'm scared."

The back of Billy's neck prickled, the sensation climbed up to his scalp. What to say? If he were in his father's place, he'd be scared, too. "I'm here, Dad."

"Yeah." Their eyes met. The man was lucid now, Billy could see. Like a face coming up from the bottom of a pool. Slowly his father lifted his hand. "What's gonna happen to you, kid? Scares me."

A fast pitch smacked into the catcher's mitt.

"How long is this gonna take?" Billy asked.

"What?" said Bonnie.

"The *game*."

The reason he'd invited her was because she seemed knowledgeable and actually thrilled when some players left an envelope with tickets for Wrigley Field. "Look at these seats!" she'd exclaimed. "My dad would go crazy!" Now she told him, "Two hours, more like three. Boy, this has been a full week for me. I've got a shift tonight, too."

He squinted at the diamond and it occurred to him that Bonnie assumed she was on the clock, right now. He was *paying* for her company. He sighed.

"Maybe I should've given your dad the tickets."

"Oh, he can't leave the house anymore. But he loves watching the games on TV. He lives for this."

Billy spied a beer vendor. "Why doesn't he leave the house?"

"He's on oxygen. He's got emphysema. Not doing well, sorry to say."

"Two beers please!" Billy called, waving. He rubbed his temple. "That's too bad."

Bonnie said quickly, "No beer for me, please."

Rather than correct himself, Billy watched the vendor pour out two tall cups. He could keep one in reserve and that would save him time later. He paid the vendor and settled back with a satisfying slurp.

"Just so you know," he said, setting the second cup at their feet, "that one has your name on it. If you change your mind."

"I don't drink anymore. I can't."

He looked at the scoreboard. Only the third inning. "That so?"

"I have a problem so I have to face it. I think people can change. Not everyone believes that. But I do, truly. Otherwise, where's hope?"

He didn't want to have this conversation. Lord. What was she, another Glitter Boy? He could use some peace. But then he noticed Bonnie's posture, her arms crossed in front of her. The determined cast of her lips.

"Doesn't it get tricky working at the club?" he asked.

"Oh, I've seen worse. It's nothing compared to Antarctica."

The crowd roared when a hard-hit line drive caromed off the wall and the runner raced around second base, attempting a triple. A headfirst slide—safe! Bonnie and Billy had risen to their feet with everyone else, and now they sat down.

"Antarctica?"

"Yeah, when I was in graduate school I volunteered at a research station. It's mainly guys down there, and in the off hours there's lots of drinking. There's not much else to do. And it's so dark. I was going to be a scientist, too. That's where I met my husband. But things got out of control."

"You're married?"

He was aware of the teeth in his brain. Nibbling at the edges. He took a long pull at his beer.

"I was. He's a botanist and an asshole. Doesn't pay his child support."

"You got a kid?"

She nodded at him like he was stupid. "I told you that when you interviewed me. It was on my application. That's why I need the second shift, since I'm home with Rory. Dad can't handle him, the condition he's in. My sister comes in most evenings. She could take Rory today because it's a Saturday."

The teeth in his brain slowly opened—a yawn—followed by a vacant belch.

"Oh yeah. Right."

Bonnie cupped her hands in front of her mouth. "Let's get a hit!"

"What's a botanist do in Antarctica?" Billy asked. "There are no plants."

"Sure there are! Lots of lichens. There's moss. Some liverworts, too."

She shook her head as if astonished by his assertion. The batter slapped a single to right field, and the man on third base scampered home. Bonnie clapped.

"Oh, of course!" he exclaimed. "Liverworts. What was I thinking?"

She flashed a smile, and Billy thought: God, she's pretty. He wanted to look under her sunglasses.

"We were specialists in paleobotany," Bonnie said. "Vascular plants were our thing. Millions of years ago, there were forests down there. All kinds of fossil angiosperm wood."

A foul ball sliced in their direction. Billy froze but Bonnie stood up and reached, hoping to snag it. The ball crashed on the steps several rows above their heads, then bounced into the hands of a happy fan.

"If I got a ball," she said, sitting down, "I'd give it to Dad, and he'd turn around and give it to Rory. He'd enjoy explaining what it meant."

Billy pondered this statement as he started his second cup of beer. It occurred to him, matter-of-factly: I'm falling in love with this person.

It was absurd.

He felt surprised, and suddenly very lonely.

In the sixth inning he went to the public restroom under the stadium deck where a line of men and boys stood in front of a long tin urinal, holding their penises, occasionally conversing over the hollow hum of liquid hitting metal.

"I feel good about today!"

"We looked better yesterday."

"I got tickets for tomorrow—anybody interested?"

Billy finished and zipped himself up. What should I say to her? he wondered. What's the right thing?

The fact that he was her boss didn't seem to make much of an impression on Bonnie. But this attitude didn't annoy him. No. Because he was *more* than a boss, right? He was a man with his own life.

The teeth in his brain, ever persistent, confirmed as much. It was hot, and he desired another beer, but he didn't want to drink it in front of her. He considered buying one under the grandstand and downing it quickly before returning to his seat, but he decided against it.

He walked forward with deliberate steps, sucking in his stomach, thinking: Damn. I look like a penguin.

"Rory loves my dad. They spend a lot of time together, he's really good about helping him with his oxygen. You know what he calls it? He calls it the 'good air.' He says, 'Grampa, you need more good air.' Sometimes I hear that and I tell myself: Yes, everybody needs more good air. There's too much of the bad stuff around us."

"That's true," Billy said.

"Arizona might be better for his health. That's what the doctors say. You know, easier to breathe. There's a clinic where I'd like to get him evaluated but he's in no shape to travel by himself. I'm saving up for this winter. I don't want to wait too long."

"No, of course not."

She touched his arm. "Thanks for bringing me here today. I should've said that earlier. There's good air at the ballpark. People talk, there's a rhythm. You watch, you listen. You learn. I look forward to telling Dad and Rory about this afternoon."

Billy experienced a sudden urge to put his arms around her. She was brave and smart and good. Who wouldn't want to hold on?

"Where do you live, Bonnie?"

"We were in Wicker Park but now we're in Avondale. Where do you live?"

"Lincoln Park," Billy replied. "Just moved in, actually. Don't know the neighborhood all that well."

He wasn't going to brag, but he'd bought himself a very nice place. The club was doing well; the bank was generous with the loan. He hadn't had time to furnish all the rooms yet, but he'd installed a hot tub, just like the fancy ones he'd heard about in California or Scandinavia—why, it was the first private hot tub in Chicago, for all he knew, and on his birthday last month he'd hosted a housewarming party and invited many people, including the Big Q's disc jockey and Glitter Boy who brought along some beautiful girls and they snorted lines of coke ("suppertime!" Glitter Boy chortled) before a performance artist with aerosol cans and cardboard stencils invited them to take off their pants, so they could have spray-on leopardskin trousers. "Don't worry, it's my own formula and it won't hurt your skin," the artist said.

A young woman laughed, shaking her hips. "It tickles!"

"Don't anyone touch it yet," the artist warned. "It'll smear. The best way to dry it is by dancing."

So they danced and danced, and Billy removed his pants and got sprayed, too.

Later in the evening, he invited girls into the hot tub, but it didn't work out the way it was supposed to. They entered the water but didn't stay with him. They complained that it was too hot, or claimed that they didn't want to damage their new paint jobs. Billy was skeptical. Late that night, after everyone had gone home, he lingered in the tub, trying to remove his spots, and he remembered his father, the vigil in the hospital, this gloomy anniversary. He blurted aloud into the air: "I'm doing the best I can!"

"Here he comes," Bonnie said. "It's Kingman!"

A buzz went through the crowd. Earlier in the game, she'd already pointed out this player, a tall man with big shoulders and a moustache. He was like a lumberjack, burly and lanky. His first time at bat, he'd struck out with mighty slashing swings. The second time he'd walked. This season, Bonnie told him, he'd hit monstrous home runs, including a shot that sailed out of the stadium and over Waveland Avenue before striking an elderly couple's front porch. His latest nickname was Kong. "Now if Dave Kingman came to the Big Q, that would be something! I'd get an autograph for Rory."

The first pitch was high and outside, ball one. The second was in the dirt, ball two. "Throw something he can swing at!" someone shouted. And the next pitch, Kingman swung. *Thwack!* A soaring fly ball brought the crowd to its feet. Billy rose with the others and then he groaned with them, too, when the ball curved foul into a distant row.

For the next pitch, Kingman took an even bigger cut, for a towering pop up that also curled foul, this time going backward, higher and higher. Billy and Bonnie tilted their heads as the ball fluttered and continued rising. He lost sight of it against the fleecy clouds.

"Where'd it go?"

"Did you see it come down?"

"No."

"With the winds off the lake," Bonnie said, "sometimes it gets weird."

"Yeah, look at the flag," pointed out a man behind them. "It's been shifting around all day. Gusts can send it anywhere."

"It's gotta come down," Billy insisted.

The next pitch, Kingman struck out.

✿

They followed the stream of spectators toward the exit. The Cubs had blown a lead and lost by five runs. Bonnie declared, "Well, we'll get them tomorrow."

The game had taken three hours, but Billy was sorry it was over. He'd enjoyed sitting next to Bonnie and pursuing a meandering conversation while a pointless and often bewildering spectacle unfolded in front of them. It felt like life itself—but grounded and temporarily contained, offering a chance to focus.

Now the prospect of another Saturday night at the Big Q loomed unappealingly. It seemed too much, too loud, too soon.

"Hey, I got an idea," he said. "Forget work. We don't have to go to the club tonight. Let's play hooky."

"How's that?"

"Let's do something else. Catch a movie. Or I could show you my new place. We could grill some steaks or something."

Bonnie laughed. "No, I don't think so."

"Why's that funny?"

"Skip work, just like that? Thanks for the ticket and everything, but it's not a good idea."

"Why not?"

She laughed again and when he stopped walking and stared, she turned serious. "Frankly, I need the hours, Billy. And if I don't show up, that leaves Lennie by himself up front on a Saturday night. If we bring in someone from the wait-staff to help at the bar, they don't know the ropes and it just passes on the problem. What if the wait-staff has a no-show? It's a mess."

Billy wasn't used to being lectured by one of his employees. But she did have a point.

"Can I at least drive you home?"

"No thanks. The number eight bus is perfect for me."

"How 'bout one of those hats for Rory?"

He pointed to a display of souvenir ballcaps. The seller, a hairy-chested man with a gold medallion, eyed them hopefully.

"Well, okay then," she said. "Thank you."

"Buy two, get the second one half-price," urged the hairy-chested man.

Billy counted out bills. "Sure, why not?"

"But I don't need two," she said.

"What about your dad?" Billy asked. "Caps aren't just for kids. You wanna bring your dad something, too."

"All right," she replied softly.

He walked her to the bus stop and, despite the crush of people, she managed to slip onto the first bus. In order to free her hands she'd pulled her long hair behind her ears—little ears, almost childlike—and placed both caps atop her head. As the bus pulled away, she smiled and waved from the window, and Billy's heart filled with gladness.

He shouldn't have invited her back to his place. That was dumb. Too soon. But the caps for Rory and her dad had been an inspiration. Instead of parting on a note of rejection, they'd shared a moment. She'd accepted an overture. He was a good guy. Yes, Bonnie thought he was a good guy. Billy headed straight to the Big Q, thinking of the future.

☼

"Come on, bring it on, bring it on!"

At one end of the dance floor, Lennie gripped a broom over his shoulder like a baseball bat and another employee, a fat kid named Chuck, made the lob. Lennie swung, and *splat!* An object sailed upward and hit the ceiling. It stuck there, next to the mirror ball, which in daylight appeared a dull orb, a dead sun. They howled in laughter—Lennie was so convulsed that he dropped the broom and fell to his knees, gripping his sides.

"What the hell is going on here?"

Billy stepped out from the booths by the fire exit.

They froze.

"And who are you?" he added, to a third kid who stood on the edge of the dance floor, clutching a bottle of beer. He wasn't an employee. The kid chewed on his lips and Lennie answered, "That's my brother."

Billy jerked his thumb toward the exit. "*Out!*" The kid obeyed immediately and Billy called after him, "and put that down!" Without breaking a stride, the boy placed the bottle on a table and disappeared through the door. Obviously a minor. Billy didn't need that kind of trouble.

Now he stepped onto the dance floor and inspected the ceiling. The sticking object appeared to be a jelly donut.

"The fuck is this?" Billy said. "Game's over. Clean it up, check the kegs and get the inventory ready. Then I'll see you in my office."

He heard a scurry of activity behind him as he headed up the stairs.

Billy was disgruntled but not surprised. It was always a good idea to come in at an unexpected hour, to see what employees got up to when you weren't around. Now he had a clear picture. Lennie was the instigator, bold enough to bring along his little brother, while Chuck, the fat kid, was pliable. He'd have to keep an eye on that weenie.

Back in the days when his father ran the Big Q as a pool hall, Billy had instigated his share of shenanigans. He'd slipped six-packs out the fire exit to high school buddies and he knew where Mack hid the collection key to the pinball machines. Billy borrowed the key periodically and filled his pockets with quarters. When his father noticed the dip in revenue, a loyal employee called Stump got blamed. An ex-marine with a protruding lower lip, Stump was a bit dim, and somehow, the more he protested his innocence, the guiltier he appeared. "I want to believe him," Mack had confided, after he fired Stump, "but the guy can't be trusted. What can I do?" Billy listened without a word. His father lived in a world where the rules were simple, as inexorable as gravity.

Now that he was in his father's position, Billy trusted no one. He'd remodeled his father's old office and installed central air conditioning, soft leather chairs and a couch. Swank and cool, Billy's office had welcomed various waitresses and female customers who'd been persuaded to come up for a drink. In the ductwork of the air conditioning, Billy had built a secret shelf where he kept an old fruitcake tin full of cash.

When he was a child, his mother had saved buttons in this tin. He'd enjoyed shaking it and listening to the rattle, then pulling off the lid to admire the colorful discs spilling out. Nowadays it contained wads of bills wrapped in rubber bands, the undeclared earnings that he skimmed from the bar till. Depending on the season and on his personal spending, there was usually between $3000 and $5000 stashed away.

A plan was taking shape in his mind. He slid back the panel and removed the tin and popped open the lid. As he fingered the money, he wondered: how much? Tens and twenties would make a thick envelope, impressive after a fashion; but his $100 bills were crisper and cleaner. And there was something jolly and reassuring about Ben Franklin's well-fed face. Yes, he would send Ben as his emissary.

His message was more delicate, though, requiring several drafts before he got it right and presentable on a fresh white page.

> *Dear Bonnie,*
>
> *Thank you for a great day. You know, I think it's time you had a vacation. Please accept the enclosed gift and take your Dad and Rory to Arizona. You deserve it. Don't worry about work. Your job will be waiting for you when you get back.*
>
> *Your friend,*
>
> *Billy*

Earlier versions had ended with "I'll miss you" or "forever yours," but he'd ruled against such wording and scratched it out. Mustn't appear too pushy. First he had to impress her as a special guy. Keep your eye on the ball, he told himself.

When she returned from Arizona, he mused, Bonnie would thank him with a tender shy gaze and he would shrug and say *Oh, it was nothing* and she would reply *But it was so good of you!* and, suddenly, breaking into a smile, Bonnie would throw open her arms and—wait, was that a knock on the door?

"Come in!"

It was Lennie.

"Inventory's fine, we're all set up for tonight. Everything's spic and span."

Billy took his time before answering. "You bring your brother here often?"

"No."

"How much does he pay for drinks? You keeping a tab?"

Lennie rubbed the side of his face. "It won't happen again."

"I have this thing about stealing, you know? Bugs the shit out of me."

Now Lennie didn't meet his eyes. Perhaps he thought he was going to be fired. But he couldn't fire Lennie, especially with Bonnie going away on vacation. He would need Lennie for extra shifts. So it was just as well for Lennie to feel that he owed him.

"We'll drop it this time," Billy said.

Lennie looked up gratefully. As he turned to leave, Billy called, "One more thing. Tonight I have some obligations so I'll be in and out of the club. I want you to give this envelope to Bonnie at midnight. You got that?"

Lennie took the envelope and nodded.

"Don't lose it. And don't forget. Midnight."

He had no intention of returning to the Big Q that evening, but if staff believed he might reappear at any moment, it kept them on their toes. Entrusting $1000 in cash to Lennie was a stretch, but tonight he would be on his good behavior. The crucial thing was the effect. It would look more noble and selfless if Billy didn't deliver the envelope himself and immediately lay claim to Bonnie's gratitude. His generosity would have time to sink in.

Besides, he was edgy and might not say exactly the right thing, he might blurt out something clumsy that would distract from the main point. Billy knew he had to be careful.

He removed a folder from his files and went straight home. He tried to keep busy by starting the charcoal and preparing his dinner. The gnawing teeth in his skull had taken a rest but now his stomach felt aflutter with the nervousness of romance, of love. While his steak sizzled on the grill, he made himself a stiff gin and tonic. He pictured Bonnie and raised his glass to the air for a toast. "*To us!*"

He sat down to his food with the folder beside him, and fished out Bonnie's original job application. The first thing he noticed was her large, bold handwriting. Very neat, with a pronounced forward slant. The fact that she'd graduated from college and started graduate school didn't appear on her application. Why was that? Was she modest? Or, on the contrary, she was proud, and unwilling to reveal everything about herself for this kind of job? Billy thought for a minute, chewing, and decided that he liked Bonnie's modesty and pride. Yes, he approved. These qualities spoke well of her.

Her birth date, though, was a surprise. He did the math—wow, she was 34 years old. She looked much younger. To be 34 and working every night with a bunch of 20 year olds at the Big Q must get tedious. Billy himself was only 29, and if it weren't for the fact that he could boss the nitwits around, he didn't think he could stand it. Did that make Bonnie an underachiever? No—no, that wasn't it. It showed grit. Yes. Bonnie had grit. Just look at how she was dealing with her drinking problem. You had to give her credit. And the fact that she looked younger than her age showed good genes, too. Because, when the time came, they would want to have a child of their own. That would be nice. And for their kid, they could certainly come up with a better name than Rory. What kind of name was that?

He cleared away his plate and took his time washing up, and then prepared himself another drink. He wished he could speed up the clock. At 10:30 he would telephone the club, he told himself, just to check in. He managed to wait till 10:20.

"Big Q!" shouted a voice over thumping disco music. "It all happens here."

It was weenie Chuck. If Bonnie had answered, he would've hung up and tried again later. "This is Billy. Everything all right?"

"Oh sure. Sure!" Chuck said. "Good crowd. Don't worry about us!"

"Put Lennie on the line, will you?"

There was a clunk and for a long minute Billy nervously shuffled his feet on the linoleum, dancing to the music on the telephone. He traced a finger on his upper lip and wondered if he should grow a moustache, a big one like Dave Kingman. Finally, Lennie: "How are you, Billy?"

"You remember what to do at midnight?"

"Right. You bet. Got it here in my pocket."

Billy made a few more inquiries, at pains to sound normal, but after hanging up, he found himself alone again with his thoughts. He finished his drink with an aggressive gulp, and the teeth in his skull made a sudden nip. Billy flinched, twisting his head to the side. Then, on an impulse, he picked up Bonnie's job application and dialed her home number. It rang nine times.

"*Hello?*"

Just one word, but this person definitely sounded like a sleepy old man. So: she wasn't lying about living with her father. He'd suspected as much but it didn't hurt to make sure. "Can I speak to Bonnie?"

"She's at work. Who is this?"

Billy pictured him in striped pajamas, a grizzled face, beneath a new Cubs cap.

"Who *is* this?" he repeated. "Listen, don't call here at this hour!" He hung up.

Geez, Billy thought. What a crabby guy.

He walked through his house, turning on lights, both upstairs and downstairs. It was more cheerful that way. Shortly after midnight, the phone rang. This is it! he told himself. Be cool. He lifted the receiver to his ear, instantly recognizing the music. "Billy here," he croaked.

"Hey man, where you been? You okay?"

The male voice caught him off balance. It was Glitter Boy.

"What do you want?"

"The big question. How's your head? Any action in there?"

"Leave me alone, will you?"

"Love is the answer," Glitter Boy said.

Billy slammed down the phone and resumed pacing. Oh, why couldn't time go faster? Then he reasoned: well, Bonnie was busy, she wouldn't call till her shift ended at two a.m. Billy made himself another gin and tonic. He wasn't sleepy. He took his glass and pushed through the screen door to his back yard.

It was a narrow, long lot, a fine yard for this part of the city. In the future he and Bonnie could throw parties here. It would be a blast! He noticed the shadowy form of his hot tub and decided to fill it now. The jewel on his crown. Why shouldn't he enjoy it?

A turn of the spigot brought a sudden rush and roar of water. This part always pleased him. From a cedar box he extracted a bottle of bubble bath. Yes—bring on the bubbles! He finished his drink and peeled off his clothes and climbed in the tub. Again he thought of Bonnie. He wanted to kiss her little ears.

He leaned back, resting his head against the edge, and sang,

> *"I'm looking over*
> *a four-leaf clover*
> *that I overlooked before!"*

He knew most of the verses. His father had sung this song. The neon shamrock was somewhere in the mildewed basement of the Big Q. Maybe he should haul it up to the office, for a laugh, for nostalgia's sake. When he plugged it in, it might still work.

"First is the sunshine,
Second the rain,
Now come the roses
that bloom in the lane!"

"Billy?"

He sat up, sloshing. "Who's there?"

"I rang the doorbell but nobody answered, and then I heard you singing out here."

Bonnie emerged from the shadows.

"I think you know why I'm here," she said.

Her sudden appearance was astonishing but it occurred to him, on top of everything else, that it was only one o'clock. She'd left work early. "Everything okay at the Big Q?" he asked.

"I can't accept this money, Billy. It makes no sense."

"Didn't you read my note? I just want to help. Your dad and all."

She came closer and momentarily stumbled—Billy had dropped his clothes on the grass, and she'd trod on them. "What the—oh my." Now he saw more than her silhouette. Light from an upstairs window softly illuminated her face.

There was a time, not long ago, when he might've added, *Hey, come in and join me. Bet you didn't have this in Antarctica!* But now he felt shy. "I wasn't expecting you, Bonnie."

"I'll leave the envelope right here, and you can get it when you come out."

"Why? Don't do that. Please. Why can't I be good to you?"

She knelt and disappeared from his line of vision, and then she stood again. "What am I supposed to think? Lennie hands me this envelope at the bar and I rip it open and everybody sees all this money in it."

"You're worried what other people think? A kid like Lennie?"

"Oh, Billy. I don't even know what I think. But a man gives something, he expects something in return. I don't want to be in a conversation like that. Where's the justice?"

He shifted, a small wave lapping at his chest. "Wow. That's kind of cynical. Wouldn't Rory enjoy a trip? I mean, in addition to your dad. What about Rory?"

"What about him? You leave Rory out of this."

Her tone was sharp.

"The envelope embarrassed you in front of other people," he continued. "Is that it? I embarrass you?"

"No, no."

"You think you're better than me? I'm not stupid, you know."

"Nobody's calling you stupid. You're out of line, all right? I'm done here." She walked away.

"No! No you aren't!"

Her voice, more distant now, from the shadows: "Yes I am! Listen, Billy. I quit. It's for the best."

"Come back here!"

But she was gone. Billy slapped the water in disgust. Why? Why did it have to be like that? He lay back in the tub and slipped below the surface. Goddamnit, this world was impossible!

Oh, to be somewhere else! To never return . . .

He stayed down a long time. Eventually he had to come up for air, though, and he broke the surface with a tremendous gasp, shaking his head and clearing his nose. His chest heaved for oxygen. *The good air.*

He was still angry, his thoughts a jumble. Before the end of summer, he'd get a girl in this hot tub and fuck her. Yes. Two girls. Fuck them both! Never mind Bonnie. She'd walked out on him. He would never forget that.

But in the next breath, he also told himself: I love her. Why?
I do.

There was no denying this admission. He wondered what his
father would say. Oh, he could hear Mack all right, when it came
to the Big Q. But what about everything else? This larger, bewildering game, his nibbled brain and liverworts in Antarctica? So
much lay ahead of him. *Dad, what next?*

Suddenly, there was a splash in the tub. Startled, he drew
back. Something had fallen in next to him. He looked from side
to side, at the trees moving in the wind, and then back at the
water. A round object bobbed to the surface. A baseball.

"What?"

His day at the stadium returned to him, the yells, a vision of
hope, mighty swings. He tilted back his head, unable to see the
clouds through the darkness.

"Oh, no way!"

He stood abruptly, water streaming, and climbed out of the
tub. He clutched at his head and stumbled naked across the grass
toward his shining empty house.

EIGHT

Parc de Vincennes, 1994

Wild West Show

Maybe you saw the game. It was on TV, if you have cable. In France. If you did, probably it didn't make much sense to you, even if you knew the rules. And if like many in the Parc de Vincennes you didn't have a clue about *those*, either, well it was simply incomprehensible. My wife Geneviève says we Americans need to grow up. The trouble started when our new pitcher, Chad Deschene, refused to wear a war bonnet. We were all warmed up, the cameras were poised, the national anthem cassette was cued in the PA system—and he pointed to the clump of feathers on the dugout bench and asked, "What's that?"

"That's for you, Chad."

He studied it for a moment, then picked it up with the tips of his fingers as one might handle a dead bird.

"For me?"

"Yeah, sure. Put it on!"

"You got to be kidding."

"It's not my idea," I told him. "It's Monsieur Chaboche. It's an honor, really. Just for the opening ceremony."

A ripple of laughter moved down the bench. Our first baseman, Fly, was stretching against the wall before taking the field, trying to get his old knees limbered yet one more time, and he said, "It doesn't mean anything, don't worry."

"You're damn right it doesn't mean anything. This is like imitation Sioux or Cheyenne. Or pure Hollywood injun, that's all it is. I'm from the Navajo nation, man. I don't wear this shit."

I sighed, wishing we could avoid this talk. There was no end to it, and nobody ever came out satisfied. "It's not political, Chad," I told him. "It's business. You said yourself that's why you're here, right?"

The umpire walked across the foul line and approached the bench, our lineup card in hand. He waved with impatience. "*On y va?*"

The players spilled out of the dugout, and Chad joined them, leaving the bonnet on the bench. I snatched it up and desperately looked round. At the bottom of the dugout steps, I grabbed Ramirez by the shoulder.

"Hector," I said. "You owe me."

"Aw, come on. You're joking."

In a second I had snatched off his cap while he laughed, shaking his head. "No laughing out there," I told him. "Serious face. Now go show them!"

He straightened the feathers. His last words before running out to join the others for the national anthem: "Now you owe me."

At least you've heard of the Paris Buffaloes? I hope so, but if not, you're hardly alone. Usually when you mention the team people say they had no idea that baseball was popular over here. Well—it's not. But we're trying. The Buffaloes are a sort of novelty; we play exhibitions against athletic clubs in other European cities. Over here baseball is a rich man's game, for people who've traveled and think it's chic. They want something different. The Buffaloes represent the sport, do clinics for kids, whatever serves our image. Our owner Chaboche has talked his way into grants from the Ministry of Sport and the Ministry of Culture, too. Franco-American goodwill and all that.

Our players include some former major leaguers, some names you'd recognize if you know your box scores and failed drug tests. By the time Chad arrived, I'd been with the organization for five seasons and had just assumed the role of player/manager, which meant all kinds of things with the Buffaloes. Chaboche needed someone who could explain the ropes to the new guys, a combination chaperon and interpreter on the cheap, someone who could play second base and also help teammates figure out a train schedule or dissuade a homesick 19-year-old from breaking his contract and jumping on the next plane to see his girlfriend Becky in Gillette, Wyoming. *That* was my job.

I also did the phone negotiations with Chad Deschene to get him over here. Chaboche had been pursuing him for over a year, eager for the team to have its very own Indian. I didn't encourage him along these lines but I wasn't the one giving orders; for Chaboche, who'd carved out a successful career in Paris real estate, American baseball was a hobby, but a hobby he pursued with great energy; it should reflect his seriousness and flair, like his other enthusiasms for hot air balloons, which he also raced, or for his model farm in La Lozère, which operated totally with period steam machinery.

Besides, we were doing Deschene a favor. He'd been released from his AAA contract and a promising career after an auto accident and repeated trips to the surgeon. His leg had struck the dashboard, shattered his kneecap. Ever since, despite operations and therapy, he'd had trouble coming down on his left leg at the end of his pitching motion, and as a result had lost his control. He still had speed, all reports said that the kid could throw a ball through a wall, but he couldn't place it. Word got around fast and opponents stopped trying to hit him; batters just protected the plate and waited out walks. In his last appearance, Chad walked six out of the last seven he faced. (The other got hit by a pitch.) Instead of sending him down, his organization cut him completely. At 22 Deschene was finished, and got a job selling satellite dishes.

That was when I started calling Phoenix. It took a number of tries to convince him, for he'd never heard of us. "Look, it's not the money, I know we can't impress you there," I admitted. "But it's the chance to get your hand in again and change your stats. Nobody's going to give you another chance till you do something about those numbers."

This argument carried the day, I could tell. No one ever wanted to finish with the Buffaloes; they always came to Europe thinking that they were just passing through. We talked about a few details, I arranged to meet him at the airport. After our last conversation, when I hung up the phone and relayed the good news to Chaboche, he said, "Ross, did you ask him about his ponytail?"

"Uh, no. I forgot."

"Well I sure hope he hasn't cut it. He looks fabulous in that Evansville roster photo. That's the one I'm sending to the press."

When I met him at Aéroport Roissy-Charles de Gaulle, he was, sorry to say, ponytail-less. On the train into the city I mentioned this fact.

"You cut your hair, I see."

"Yeah. It was easier that way at my new job. *Old* job, I should say, the one I just quit. I wasn't cut out for sales."

"You still in shape? You've been training?"

"A little," he replied, not too convincingly. I was relieved, though, to see he had kept a trim bodyweight—that would be a consolation to Chaboche. I was the only one besides the boss to know that we had a discrimination policy on this club against big guys. It was both aesthetic and a reflection of the European market, which had a hard time accepting chunky athletes. On more than one occasion we'd let good talent get away from us simply because the player in question was a fat boy. And once we'd refused to renew the contract of a first baseman because in the two years he'd been with us, he'd put on thirty pounds. He'd proved incapable of adapting to French ways, and instead of eating French food which, despite its multi-course meals and fearlessness of butter, would keep a person in form, as long as you respected its logic and rhythm, he nostalgically went day after day to fill up on American-style burgers on the Champs-Elysées; and instead of working out in his free time, which was absolutely necessary since over here we rarely scheduled more than two games a week, he sat around on café terraces, drinking beer. It was hard for some new arrivals to understand, that working less required discipline. They couldn't handle it, having always known a day-to-day grind. Soon his gut hung over his belt, and from that point it didn't matter how far he could hit the ball, because as far as we were concerned, he was unwelcome. Chaboche had a favorite joke about this subject which he trotted out at sports banquets and fundraisers. Once there was a young player in the American heartland (*l'Amérique profonde!*) who showed a lot of potential, who was beginning to attract attention far beyond his small college team. One day before a game his coach took him aside and said that the legendary scout, Old Marv, was in the stands, he'd driven 400 miles to see him. This was his big chance. So the young player ran onto the diamond and played his heart out. His first three times at bat, he slapped hits. He stole two bases. On the field he made diving catches, and threw out a runner at home. And his last time at the plate, he cracked a home run off the scoreboard to win the game. Broke the scoreboard. His teammates carried him on their shoulders off the field. Then the coach came running up, calling Wait, Wait! Old Marv was asking for him. They let him down. He went over to the stands where Old Marv was sitting in his famous wrinkled brown suit. "You wanted to talk to me?" the young player says. Old Marv nods. "Yep, I have to tell you, that was a hell of a game. One of the best I ever saw." The young player shrugged and nodded at the same time, but didn't say anything. Waiting. Then Old Marv added, "You know, I could almost offer you a contract." The young player looked up. "*Almost?*" "Yeah, but I can't," Old Marv said. "Why not?" the young player asked, crestfallen. Old Marv replied: "Well—because your butt isn't big enough. Sorry, kid."

This went down a storm with Europeans, got a big laugh every time, for this is how they saw American baseball players. Once I was sitting with guests from an American engineering firm doing business in France, a potential sponsor for the team, and I translated this joke. They were appalled. The more I tried to explain, the touchier they became, and eventually I gave up. As my wife Geneviève says, it's only a game. And she doesn't mean just baseball.

The first inning, Chad looked good. He didn't give up any hits and walked only one. He struck out a batter and it was obvious that our opponents, the Munich All-Stars, weren't used to seeing so much speed. When we came off the field to take our first at-bat, there was an optimistic feeling in the air, and it wasn't just me, it was everybody. "Okay, let's put something on the board!" I called, and gave a clap. A few Buffaloes joined in and we got some talk going.

Ramirez was our lead-off man, and the second pitch he hit a single up the middle, nice as could be. Now the bench grew livelier, and one of our outfielders, Will Clayton, said, "Must've been the feathers that done it."

This got a laugh, but I don't know if Deschene heard the remark. Or if he would care. I simply hoped we could put the incident behind us, and play. Probably most of the people at the park didn't notice the switch; the numbers on our uniforms appeared on the sleeve, and were too small to see from afar; they only served as reference on the field, for the umpires, while the scorer sat near the dugout. In place of numbers, our shirts displayed our sponsor's mineral water logo of big blue mountains. Anyone watching in the stands would assume that the guy in the headdress must be the new Indian recruit, and think no more; and if people who saw close-ups on TV got confused once the game started (Ramirez and Deschene didn't resemble each other very much—Ramirez was darker, probably closer to how local viewers expected an Indian to appear, anyway), even then, maybe that wasn't a problem. So what if people asked questions? Just as long they talked, that's what Chaboche wanted. Publicity. Maybe I could tell the boss I'd done it on purpose.

While I was mulling this over, our next batter, Jerry Carter, hit a slow infield bouncer, and Ramirez slid hard into second base to break up a potential double-play. In addition to taking out the shortstop, though, he took himself out, too. When the dust settled, he didn't get up, but remained in the dirt, clutching his ankle.

The bench fell silent. "Oh, for Christ's sake." I threw up my hands and ran out onto the field to see what was the matter.

Ramirez looked up with as much disgust as pain when I reached him. He said simply, "Yeah, I think so."

"Gilles isn't here today," I told him.

"I know," he said.

Gilles was our trainer, a doctor and a good one but since he was a volunteer, you couldn't expect him to come to every game. Today his daughter had a school program or something.

I helped Ramirez limp off the field and sent in Wilson as a pinch runner. I didn't pay much attention to the rest of the inning because I was getting a bucket of ice—in Gilles' absence I do my share of hands-on nursing—but we managed to push across a run, so Chad Deschene went back out to the mound with a lead.

"Okay, fella, put 'em away!" I called from my position at second base, but he made no sign to anyone around him. He was nervous, we could see, and immediately he fell behind the first batter. The Munich All-Stars included some players who were actually German, including the big guy at the plate now, a player named Scherer who'd learned the game growing up near a military base. He was good, a better hitter than some of our Buffaloes. Chad was lucky to get him to chase a bad pitch and pop it up. The next batter he walked, and then the next. By then I felt I had little choice but to call for time, go over to the mound and try to settle him down with a little chat. Not that there was much to say.

"Don't tire yourself early, pal."

"I'm not tired. I feel good. Don't worry about me. Really."

"Well, you're using a lot of pitches. Let them hit it, we'll do the work."

They scored twice before we escaped, and the next three innings were more of the same. Deschene threw and threw; for brief patches he seemed to regain his control, and looked great;

there was one clutch strike-out with the bases loaded that was a beauty. But it became obvious that accuracy wasn't his only problem; his concentration was unraveling, too. This put me in a tight spot. Mike Coontz was the only pitcher I had left, because Ricardo Milon still had a blister and the previous week we'd fired Randy Sharman from the team for habitual drunkenness. And I'd lost my main reliever the previous month during our tour of Spain, a series of exhibitions traveling by bus, to play the same so-called Spanish club in every town, a line-up actually stacked with Cubans, who kicked our ass every night. It was like a recurring nightmare. We lost three players on that trip, guys who either couldn't take it or who got too sick from some peanut butter Carter had brought over from America that had gone rotten in the heat. It smelled like rubber gloves, and they ate it anyway. Players falling to their knees and throwing up along the third base foul-line, and on the bus . . . oh, I was still trying to forget that trip!

"Why do you put up with it?" Geneviève asked me. "Ross, when are you going to call it quits?"

She wasn't unsympathetic, but she had a real job with AC-TEL and didn't see the point of my contortions. She was also tired of the Buffaloes being on the road so much.

"You know how it is," I told her, "things could change again soon. What else can a guy like me do in this country?" Then I reminded her of the favors Chaboche had performed in getting our papers straightened out so we could be married. "Honey, we owe him."

A couple of days before Chad's first game, Chaboche arranged a meeting with the media. It was an impressive affair, held in the reception area of the Hôtel Troilus, with most of the press, and a fair amount of Parisian radio and television stations present. It was intended to make Chad feel welcome, show him that his arrival was appreciated. At the lunch before the meeting, I had a premonition that maybe we were going too far. Chaboche was all pleasantness, glowing over his new recruit, full of praise for his prospects, and telling him at length about the media coverage he was going to get. Though he didn't mention the ponytail (in keeping with my advice), he told him several times what a handsome young man he was. Chad smiled and nodded and all the while struck me as very young. Chaboche wasn't telling the entire story, either. The media conference had little to do with baseball or Chad's future pitching contribution—ordinarily we couldn't dream of this kind of coverage. In truth they were coming out of curiosity and as a follow-up to the story that had broken the previous January, concerning our first baseman, Fly.

January is when most new Buffalo recruits arrive. There's a lot of paper shuffling involved, but Chaboche had a deal at the préfecture that gave our new guys an extra-territorial derogation for work permits—a legal sham, one of his masterpieces. We hustled them from office to office through the formalities, and once everything was in order, the team would head out for training, usually in North Africa, where it was warm and we could use facilities on military bases for cheap, and the local scene different enough for the players that they stuck together.

Fly, whose real name was Phil Grimke, had just arrived in Paris. He was one of our more mature players, 36, 37 years old. He'd spent eleven years in the majors before injuries ruined him. Unlike Chad Deschene he still had both kneecaps, but he'd long since misplaced his cartilage. He'd had more operations than he admitted to. Scouts had marked him as untouchable. We signed him cheap. It was unseasonably cold for Paris that time of year, below freezing, and for some reason Fly was walking on his gimpy legs in the Bois de Boulogne. Maybe it was to slip away from his teammates, all those kids getting rowdy—the Buffaloes stayed at the Villa Saint Martin, a nice situation that Chaboche had arranged but a lot of togetherness—or maybe Fly was more than a little curious about the Brazilian transvestites in the Bois. They were one of the first things he asked me about in the train from the airport. At any rate, Fly was limping along the edge of an artificial lake, a bitterly cold day, when suddenly a woman began to scream. He stopped; she was shouting toward the trees, then she turned to the lake. There, on the ice, lay a baby on its back. It wiggled its hands and feet in the air.

Fly approached her but at the sight of him she shouted and parried with an empty baby stroller. "What is it?" he said. "How did it get there?"

She didn't understand him, and he didn't understand her, but the problem was pretty obvious. Someone had pushed the baby onto the ice. It had slid to a stop a good 20 feet from the bank. And now it lay on its back like an overturned beetle, twitching its limbs at the clouds. He could hear it crying. As soon as the woman understood that Fly wasn't another assailant, she ignored him and called to the baby, testing the edge of the ice with her foot. It broke right through; Fly grabbed her arm to keep her from falling as she called to the baby again.

Fly told her in English that he would try and he bent low and began, slowly, to slide out onto the lake on his stomach. By now other passersby had stopped to watch. He had scarcely stretched out the whole length of his body when the ice buckled and broke under him. Onlookers cried out, they thought he was in big trouble, but Fly discovered, as he flailed to take hold of the ice edge, that his feet touched bottom. The water was only waist deep, anyway. So he kept going, hacking with his fists and breaking his way through the lead-colored ice and freezing slush—probably one of the few waking hours that he no longer felt the pain in his knees!—and came closer to the baby. Here, though, the lake bottom sloped down, the water grew deeper. Soon it was up to his chin, and the baby was still out of reach.

Maybe he would've turned back right there, but later he told me the difference was, all those people were watching. He could hear their voices behind him, a lot of French swirling around his head, which he didn't understand but believed was encouraging. He tried to tread water and break ice at the same time, to bob, though by now lifting his arms had become difficult, in his sodden clothes. His next step took him too far down so he grabbed hastily at the edge. There was a *snap* like breaking a gigantic slate and, with horrible slowness, a large lozenge of ice tilted up at an angle, with the baby on it. The baby spun halfway round, then began to slide toward the water. Fly went under the surface, too deep here, then pushed himself up again, made a lunge, snagged the speeding baby with his big right hand like the great first baseman he always believed he was, and turned, began thrashing his way back to shore.

So Fly was a hero. An overnight star, with no exaggeration. There were television guest spots, interviews, the best publicity the Buffaloes ever had. Chaboche was over the moon about it, and kept Fly in the hospital for two extra days, saw to it that even in bed, he wore his cap with the Buffaloes' insignia, which appeared in every photo. That was how the club turned a corner and started making money on promotional gear. Almost immediately the story took a political slant, because it turned out the mother was Algerian, while Fly was Black—and the two young crazies who'd pulled the baby from the stroller and slid it out onto the ice were described in the media as probable skinheads (though how anyone could know is hard to guess, since the mother said her attackers wore stocking caps). The Prime Minister and the Minister of the Interior both went on the record about their shock and dismay.

Fly, to his credit, handled himself with grace during the interviews and with his interpreters. What are you supposed to do when within three days of your arrival in a country where you don't speak the language, you find yourself on the front page, heralded as a symbol of anti-racist Progress and a defender of Motherhood, and are asked to comment on the North-South divide and religious integrism? Fly smiled and said he did what he had to do, he cut right through the politics. Chaboche postponed our winter training a couple of weeks in order to fit in more television appearances.

Chad Deschene knew nothing of this, that Antoine Hubert of *Le Monde* was more likely to ask him about deforestation or genocide than his fastball. I was nervous about Chad's inexperience compared to Fly, who'd been talking to reporters for years, and smoothly adapted to the curious mixture of flattery and condescension of French intellectuals. He used them as much as they did him. Such savvy wasn't something you could expect of someone so young: Chad might actually believe that they cared about him; or, on the other hand, he might tell them to Fuck Off. In either case it would go hard on him.

"Those people owe us," Chaboche said. "He'll be all right."

I didn't see how he could be so sure, since courting intellectuals was an even more circusy enterprise than running the Buffaloes. My time in France had led me to conclude that these people were smart but in a performing animal sort of way: they thought the world revolved around their trick. Our best insurance lay in the fact that many of them were my boss's former school pals. Sometimes it was easy for me to forget but Chaboche was from an extremely competitive school, one of the best in the nation, where he'd studied economics; unlike many of his peers he hadn't gone on to be a member of Parliament or a jurist or a media commentator, but like virtually everyone in his class, he'd never paid a parking ticket.

"Is this live?" Chad whispered to me as we approached the microphones, cameras clicked and flashed, the monitor light glowed red.

"Naw," I told him as we took our chairs, "it isn't even real."

Chad was sandwiched between Chaboche and me, so I could translate the questions into English for him, while Chaboche re-layed Chad's answers back into French. It started easily enough, with "Is this your first time in this country?" and "What is your dream as a sportsman?" Chad didn't forget to smile, his voice displayed only the slightest of tremors and his replies were fine, if a little brief; Chaboche fleshed them out in his translation. Then came the serious stuff: "What new agreements would you sug-gest the American government undertake toward your indige-nous people?" and "Did you have no choice but to pursue your career outside its jurisdiction?" For the first of these Chad hes-itated for a moment, but quickly recovered: "Well, uh—they could begin by respecting the old agreements." For the second he merely shrugged and said, "Yeah."

The questioners scribbled away on their pads. They asked him about his last name, with the transparent hope that he might also have some French ancestry; but he replied that he didn't think so. ("Still, it might be possible!" Chaboche ad-libbed.) Then he made his first real gaffe by revealing that his first name had been chosen by his mother after a character from her fa-vorite TV soap opera.

This got a laugh, and not the right kind; the journalists' tone needed no translating. Chad hunched a little behind the micro-phones, and waited for the next question. Someone threw out in

English, "You don't really look like an Indian." Chad shot back, "You don't look like an idiot."

Chaboche's hand went quickly around Chad's shoulder, and he cut in: *"He is, he most definitely is, and we have proof."*

What on earth he meant by this, I had no idea. In any event, Chad's retort had been understood without translation by most of those present and it got another laugh, a more sympathetic one this time. It was true that these people were better than Americans at tolerating a little salt; they didn't expect only nicey-nice. Still, both Chaboche and I could see that Chad was tiring, and we'd better get him off. Chaboche asked the next question himself. "You like the girls here, don't you, Chad?"

Chad turned to him in bewilderment, then Chaboche leaned into his microphone and said that his new boy hadn't wasted any time getting to know the young ladies of this country, who seemed to appreciate him, too. This brought a friendly titter, and Chaboche gave a closing wave. "Thank you very much! We hope to see you there on Saturday when Monsieur Deschene shows his prowess against the Munich All-Stars!"

❄

Sixth inning, Chad on the mound with the bases loaded. We'd done some scoring ourselves, hit the ball well—I had a double—and now we led, 6 to 5. Though the bases were full, there were two outs, and Chad was ahead on the count, 1-2. I truly believed he might pull out of it. He seemed to be bearing down. I made no sign toward the bullpen.

The next pitch, though, Chad threw over our catcher Manny, over the umpire. He damn near threw it over the screen. Afterward, in the ensuing infield fire drill, he raced forward and covered the plate exactly as he should—the manager in me appreciated his execution—but by the time Manny found the ball and threw it back, two runs had scored, and we were losing the game.

He disposed of the next batter but when we returned to the dugout the frustration in the air was palpable; I could've reached out with my fingers and pinched it. "Okay, there's still plenty of time, we can get it back!" I said, pacing down the length of the bench. Everyone looked hot and angry. It wasn't just losing that was irritating; it was the way we were losing, and to whom. The Munich All-Stars, we'd had ample opportunity to observe all afternoon, were shit. They truly were. And yet, on our only appearance on TV this year, they were ahead of us. They hadn't really been able to swing against Chad—if you looked at the column, they'd managed only three hits. But combined with all the walks and an outfield error, and last inning's chaos, the score told the story. We were beating ourselves. It was time to take measures.

"Deschene, you're too tired," I told him, and called down to Coontz. "Get loose, you're on next inning."

Chad looked none too happy, but he didn't speak. I had nothing else to add. A tough outing, discouraging, but hardly the first time any of us had seen such a thing. It was only when Mike Coontz made a remark that Chad reacted. Most of us heard it, though he was talking to Ron Johnson next to him. "I guess that's all for the wild Indian," he said.

Now this is where things fell apart. Geneviève says she doesn't get it, we're all too touchy, and to this day I'm convinced it was less politics than fatigue and frustration, though Chad says the contrary, that he's had a bellyful of hearing what I think, anyway. All I know is that Chad leaped up off the bench and kicked a clipboard out of his way and went over to Coontz. "What did you say?"

The game had resumed, Morris was batting, and I ordered, "Sit down and watch, Chad."

He repeated himself. "What did you say?"

"I was just bullshitting," Coontz told him. "Let me by."

Coontz had picked up his glove and wanted to warm up, but Deschene blocked his way.

"Sit down, Chad."

"This man is not replacing me," he said.

Now I had to go over to them. "It's already decided. Now sit down. And you," I told Coontz, "keep your fucking mouth shut."

Deschene didn't move, and Ron Johnson slid off to the side, making room. Meanwhile, on the field, Morris was already out, Clark was batting, and no one in the dugout was even paying attention. Everyone was watching Deschene and Coontz, to see who would throw the first punch.

"I don't care," Chad told me, "he's not taking the field for me. Come on," he kept at Coontz, "what did you say?"

Now my temper flared. "Well look who's running the show! For your information, Deschene, he's the only pitcher we got right now. Not that you'd know, being you just arrived."

"I said," Coontz uttered in a low voice, "that's all for you, pal. You're done."

What followed was an unhistoric, pointless scuffle, in which no punches were thrown—those of us around quickly saw to that. If either had really wanted to get physical it would've been harder to control, but it was just for show, for pride. As I stepped between I thought: *I am too old for this.* By the time we settled, and everyone sat down, Clark had struck out and Wineland popped up his first pitch. We were supposed to take the field again.

Chad picked up his glove. "Hey, where do you think you're going?" I called to him.

"But Coontz hasn't even warmed up," said Fly.

I didn't like Fly meddling in my business—he could save his elder statesman pose for later—and Coontz liked it even less.

"Who's in charge here, dude?" he asked. "Not *you*."

I was sick of Coontz, though. "No, and not you, either. He's right. You're not ready. Why don't you make yourself useful and fetch Ramirez a Coke?'

Ramirez, who'd sat silently through all the fuss with his foot in a bucket of ice, suddenly lit up. "Thanks! But I'd prefer an Orangina."

We left the dugout and I cut in front of Chad on his way to the mound. "You heard me, fella. You're not on."

"Who, then? You tell me."

I hesitated for a moment. "Me."

It wasn't my plan, but I didn't see any other way out. I informed the plate umpire of the line-up switch. As I took my first and final warm-up throws from the mound, I felt like the last of the Buffaloes. I'd pitched batting practice before, in my various roles on the team, but this was hardly the same thing. Quite consciously I did not look anywhere in the direction of the first tier box, where Chaboche and his friends would be sitting. Geneviève, if she'd managed to endure the TV this long, was probably thinking: *Why didn't he tell me?* I tried to keep my expression as blank as possible. Before the first Munich All-Star stepped up to the plate, my catcher Manny came out to see me with a big smile on his face.

"You want signals?" he asked.

"Sure. Don't know that it'll make much difference."

We settled on a couple, then a guy named Holger came up to swing. My first pitch was wide, the next he fouled back. The next he swung way ahead of, and ticked a little infield pop-up that I caught myself. One down.

The next batter flied out to center. The initial *crack* gave me a sickening feeling in my stomach, but I turned and saw that it was playable. Two down.

The third batter took an eternity. He fouled and fouled, I threw a couple in the dirt, eventually ran the count full. Once I paused to wave Chad back; he'd replaced me at second base, and was playing so shallow that I had the impression he was creeping up on me, as if to reclaim the mound. "Deeper," I said. Then I threw, the hitter took a ferocious cut—and missed. My first strike-out.

Back in the dugout there was much laughter. It was exactly the opposite atmosphere of the previous inning, and I was glad for the change in mood, though I hadn't intended to accomplish it by comic relief. "So that's what the fuss was about," joked Wineland. "You just wanted to be on TV."

"Well," said Fly dryly, "looks like they can't hit your change-ups."

It was true. After Chad's considerable speed, my style had put them off balance. A 75 mile-per-hour fastball required a little adjustment. That same inning I had a turn to bat but didn't help my cause, grounding out, but a short time later Jerry Stevens hit a home run with a runner on base, and that put us ahead, 8 to 7. All very encouraging, but when we went into the eighth inning, I felt nervous, much more than earlier. Now there was a lead to protect—and I'd had time to think about things.

So had the Munich All-Stars. On the second pitch, their lead-off man slammed the ball deep to left field, and it took a fine running catch by Clark to make the out. When the ball came back to me, I gripped it hard, to keep my hand from shaking. The next batter was big Scherer again. He looked happy to see me. I tried to keep it low, and threw the first one in the dirt. He gazed back at me, waiting. The second pitch got away from me completely and I hit him.

It wasn't intentional, and he knew it, but as he trotted toward first base he made an exaggerated grimace, rubbing his arm where the ball had struck him, feigning pain. Mocking my lack of speed in front of everyone. He was big, he was smart, he was an asshole. And this was a new situation for me, a runner on base. I threw once to Fly, to hold Scherer there.

The next hitter was left-handed, and went to a 2-1 count, fouling back once. My last pitch I regretted the moment it left my hand. It was fat, no movement on the ball: straight out of batting practice. And when the batter swung, he connected full wood. He hit a shot, a vicious line drive that didn't rise—a white blur down the first base line. Fly lunged with his extended glove, caught it, and managed to keep the glove on his hand. Then he stepped back on the base to double up Scherer. I was watching over my shoulder, for I still hadn't had time to turn my body around. With a flick of his wrist, and without looking back, Fly rolled the ball toward the mound, and limped off the field, since the inning was over. He left the rest of us standing there.

There was a hesitation, then a smattering of applause from the stands. Not the roar that the play deserved. It happened so fast, many probably missed it.

This time, back in the dugout, it was quiet, too. There was none of the earlier joking or teasing. I felt embarrassed, but there was nothing I could say. Clark stepped up to the plate for us, and Ron Johnson cupped his hands, called, "All right, we need a few insurance runs!"

Coontz rose to his feet. At first I thought he was coming over to see me, and I hated him for it. But he stopped a couple of yards away, and spoke to Chad where he sat on the bench.

"Listen, you don't want us to lose, do you?"

Deschene made no reply. The phone began to ring at the end of the dugout, and the only person it could be was Chaboche. Good God, I thought. Everywhere I turn, a vote of confidence.

"Get that, will you?" I called to Wineland.

"I'm sorry, all right?" said Coontz. "How long do I have to say it?"

Chad squinted at him. "How *long?*"

Wineland called down the bench, "It's for you, Coach."

Deschene said to me, "Do you think you can go on like that?"

"What does it look like, Chad?"

He sighed. "Okay—enough. But don't expect me to act noble about this, or to go away. That's not how I do things. And you— just leave me alone," he said to Coontz.

Before I took the phone, I told Coontz to start warming up. Exercised my authority. Then I spoke into the receiver, "Allo, Guillaume? Ça va?"

Chaboche was annoyed. He didn't like to wait.

"We can't believe our eyes up here! What *are* you doing?"

It wasn't the first time he'd been confounded by our American ways. All I could do was try to put a plausible face on things.

"Don't worry. It's—it's our experiment."

❁

So the game was won by the home team. (That's us, in case you . . .) Can't say it changed the world. The overwhelming sentiment when we boarded the team bus to leave the Parc de Vincennes was not one of celebration; it was one of relief. Anger, though, seemed to have drained. Everybody was weary.

Usually on the bus after everyone's seated I stand up and make a few remarks, just to sum up the game, and congratulate those who did well. It's an old custom. Today I didn't feel like congratulating anyone, least of all myself. I was ready to skip it.

But when I climbed on the bus, I felt them watching me, expecting something. For a moment I considered ignoring them and telling the driver to start but then I wondered if they would think I was ashamed, or afraid. And that rankled me, because even with all our mistakes, I was neither. Call it foolish, Geneviève, but I still took the Paris Buffaloes seriously.

All those faces. Some looked friendly—but others, not so friendly. And they were waiting. Now I would have to find something true. My mind knew no reassuring words. Eventually I told them, "Was that really who we are? You know we can do better." I cleared my throat. "Damn it, use your imaginations." Then I took my seat and like the rest of them stared straight ahead.

NINE

San Jose, 2009

The Promise

In his mind Harold prepared a speech. If Maggie was going to fire him for stealing food, well, OK, it might've happened but he'd never gone overboard, see, and he supposed he wasn't the only one? (Of course he wasn't, but Harold wouldn't rat on other kitchen workers—these people had families to feed, and some had no legal papers.) Plus, he never called in sick. "A person can count on me!" Maggie was young for a day manager, a perky white kid with a gummy smile, hard to read. Harold felt nervous as he approached her. The pressure never let up, as much as in the days when he'd had a stadium of 50,000 people cheering him on, loving him but also daring him to fail.

"You want to see me?"

Maggie cracked a roll of nickels against the cash register drawer, then spilled the coins into their slot. With her hip, she banged the drawer shut.

"Good news, Harold."

"What's that?"

"Looks like you're in for a promotion."

What this meant, Harold had no idea. He hadn't applied for anything. But he showed no emotion.

"That so? What kind of promotion?"

"Not sure. But they want to see you at the main office at two o'clock tomorrow. Mr. Cusik himself. I'll get somebody to cover your shift."

"Cusik? You serious?"

Maggie laughed. "Must be nice to have connections."

✵

Harold had heard the stories. Cusik had bought the restaurant on a whim. He wasn't a restaurateur at all but a tech millionaire whose headquarters occupied the 18th floor of an office building barely a mile away. A frequent customer, he was fond of the stir-fry shrimp and Japanese green beans. He kept odd hours and often arrived late. Since Harold worked the day shift, he'd never seen the man, but people said Cusik walked with crutches, accompanied by an assistant who drove him the short distance from his headquarters and sat at the same table but did not eat. The story went that one night, Cusik came in late and the hostess on duty, who was new to the job, refused to serve him. The kitchen was closed, sorry. Cusik insisted that he'd arrived at this hour on other occasions and been served shrimp and beans, but the hostess stood firm. Too late, she said. Cusik became angry and, depending on whom you believed, he used foul language or even swung a crutch at her. He'd shouted, "*It's never too late!*"

Not long after this scene, employees learned the restaurant had been sold. The buyer, they discovered, was Cusik. The hostess who'd refused him was promptly fired. Everyone worried about what would happen next, but in fact almost nothing changed, except now the kitchen was kept open till two a.m., like the bar. Cusik rarely arrived to eat before midnight, often the only customer in the place while a bored night crew hung around, scrolling through their cell phones.

❁

Harold rolled up with a reverberating growl: his muffler was shot. The Toyota was a shitbox with 140,000 miles and rust, and Harold performed countless mean economies to maintain it. Without it, he couldn't get to work. He would end up on the street again. The parking lot for the main office building was located immediately off the highway, surrounded by high, manicured shrubs. Harold had no trouble finding a space, slipping in between a pair of scooters. There were many bikes and scooters in the lot.

Harold exited the elevator on the 18th floor and the receptionist instructed him to wait. True, he was ten minutes early. He sat in a leather chair with a tubular steel frame. Not uncomfortable, but it obliged an upright posture as if he was sitting in church. Harold wore his best pants and a clean white shirt, wondering if he should've put on a tie. Observing a giant ceramic sculpture of an avocado near the elevator, he reflected that the owner of such a piece, which must've cost thousands of dollars, wasn't going to be impressed by a tie. Wearing one might even count against him. Hell, what did such a guy expect from a 45 year-old dishwasher?

"Mr. Cusik is ready to see you."

She opened the door and Harold stepped into a large office. The door clicked behind him. Cusik stood facing the window, his back to Harold, propped on crutches. The window offered a sweeping view.

"Mr. Hines. Good to see you!"

"Hello."

Now Harold realized that Cusik wasn't looking out the window but was observing his reflection on the glass. Their eyes met. With surprising agility Cusik spun around and pointed a crutch.

"Sit down, please."

Harold settled into a leather chair, a larger version of the one in the waiting area. Cusik drew up to his desk but remained standing, leaning forward on the crutches.

"I've got plans for you, Mr. Hines."

"Glad to hear it."

Harold didn't bend back his neck to look up at his employer but he was mindful of his own face, a mask of unrelenting pleasantness. There was a silence as Cusik stared. Harold waited.

"Have you read much Rousseau? Do you know *The Confessions*?"

"Uh, no. Not really."

Another silence.

"Can I offer you a drink? I can get Tina to bring in a nice cold beer. With a lime, if you like."

"No thank you."

"Or maybe you prefer the finer stuff? I've got some very special single malt in a drawer here."

"No. I'm good."

Cusik came around his desk, thumping as he went. He was a slight man with a conspicuous round head, shaved perfectly smooth.

"We're going to get you out of the kitchen. Recently I looked at the payroll, you know, to better acquaint myself with the restaurant. Improve efficiencies. And your name jumped out at me. Harold Hines! We've got to give him a fair shake! Right? I'm sure you agree."

Now Cusik stood so close that he was hard to see. His belt was a chocolate-stippled leather.

"I agree," said Harold.

"So tell me. How would you like to manage the bar? Our staff is pretty solid, overall. You'd have to track the schedule, keep people on their toes. And of course you'd be in charge of inventory."

"Manage the bar? Me?"

"You'll make three times what you do now."

In the window, high cottony clouds moved across the sky. Harold knew what he had to say.

Even so, a vision unfurled before him: a chance to move out of his sublet, to get a handle on his debts, fix up the Toyota—hell, forget the Toyota, he'd get another car! Above all, he could stop looking over his shoulder. People said you couldn't buy dignity but an extra 20 bucks an hour would be a down payment on some peace of mind.

Rehab hadn't always worked for Harold, the endless meetings, the appeal to a higher power which remained a struggle; but he'd learned this much: he wasn't a person who should spend time in a bar among drinkers. There was no way around that fact. The knowledge that Cusik had a bottle of scotch at his fingertips and one syllable (*Yes!*) would set him up with a lovely drink and even an excuse—they could toast his promotion!—this possibility, in all its dubious splendor, brought a familiar anticipatory buzz in his head. How easy it would be to flip the Off Switch and forget everything he'd learned! So before it was too late he spoke in a loud voice, louder than the buzz, addressing himself as much as Cusik.

"No. Thank you, but no. I can't take that job."

"But why not?"

There was only one answer. The truth. This much, too, Harold knew. So, briefly and bluntly, he explained how his personal situation was incompatible with Cusik's offer.

"A pity."

"But I'd gladly consider other offers," Harold continued. "I'm fourteen months sober now. I'm open to suggestions. I mean it!"

It didn't matter if it sounded like he was sucking up, because the stakes ran deeper than such considerations—actually, it was the opposite of sucking up. He'd revealed himself. Announced his vulnerability. That wasn't easy. And now, he must continue to be brave. He had the man's ear.

"Give me a chance to show you what I can do."

Cusik bobbed his head. "Well. Since you put it that way. Come around here. Bring your chair."

Cusik thumped back to his desk, swiveled and sat down on his chair. He dropped his crutches to the floor. Harold carried his chair to the other side. Cusik switched on his computer, opening files, then clicked on a video game. He plugged in a console with a toggle switch. "You ever play this one?" he asked.

Home Run Derby!

Harold shook his head. He kept his eyes on the screen, resisting the urge to stare at Cusik. Who was this nut?

Cusik opened a desk drawer and extracted a baseball cap. He put it on. He brought out another cap and handed it to Harold who, when he saw the insignia, felt a panicky rumbling in his gut. "Go ahead," Cusik said. "Put it on. I'll show you how to play."

The game was simple, with pitches fired at various speeds: fastballs, looping curves and sliders. Working with the toggle, Cusik smacked a few over the fence before he eventually struck out.

"Your turn."

Harold took the toggle. The last time he'd gamed was two Christmases ago, with his son Damon from his third marriage, back when he still had visitation rights. Damon preferred games with submarines and giant sea serpents. Not baseball. Harold leaned forward and focused on the screen.

A pitch sailed at him. He swung and missed. Another pitch: he missed. He managed a foul tip. Then he struck out. He released the toggle but Cusik encouraged, "That's OK, try again. You'll get the hang."

Harold didn't want to continue but he turned back to the screen. And now, as pitches whizzed by, Cusik offered his opinions. "*You're too anxious*" and "*The best hitters are patient.*" This was especially irksome. But it also occurred to him, as he hunkered down, that maybe *this* was his new job. Right now, was he on the clock? A paid playmate for a rich loon? Harold struck out four times in a row (the pitches were programmed to go faster and faster, impossible to hit), then he released the toggle. "Sorry, Mr. Cusik. Don't think I can do this one."

"You're pathetic, Hines."

Harold raised his voice. "The fuck do you know? I played the real game, which is more than most people can say. Not this kiddie stuff."

Cusik looked at him calmly. "You don't recognize me, do you?"

Harold eyed him. Such a big, babyish head.

"No, I don't."

"I'd thought you might, Harold. But you never could come through in the clutch."

If not for this final jibe, he would've told Cusik to screw himself. He would've left the office and assumed that he'd talked himself out of a job and that he was back on the street. Bad, all around— but he'd seen worse.

Instead, he stayed on the 18th floor, watching as Cusik opened a drawer, extracted a bottle of scotch. He poured generously. Harold carried his chair to the other side of the desk, where he wouldn't have to smell the drink.

"So what's this all about? Do you know me?"

"You promised me, big time."

"What? When?"

"You abused me, and I've never forgotten."

Harold was speechless. Yes, the guy was crazy. But he seemed to believe his words. Worse, he might repeat them to other people. At the same time, Harold had the impression that Cusik wasn't angry. He was enjoying himself.

"Think back now. The pediatrics unit at St. Jude's Hospital?"

Harold shook his head. "What?"

"You don't even remember!"

Harold ran his hand along the grain of Cusik's desk. "You'd better just come out and say it."

"You promised me that you would get a hit. Then you bent over my bed and winked. '*How about a homer?*' You don't remember that?"

Suddenly—oh God—Harold could see it. Memories rushed back. Flustered, he blurted, "You must mean Riverside Hospital."

Cusik shook his head. "No, it was St. Jude's. I ought to know. I was there for a year."

Harold closed his eyes. He and his teammate, Alfredo Cruz, had visited several hospitals, they were a blur, speaking to sick children. They signed autographs and handed out tiny flashlights and other cheap swag with the team logo. Harold and Alfredo had the same agent, Arnie Swanson, who set up these encounters. "Community service is good for the kids and good for the team image and good for you when you negotiate your next contract. It's a win-win-win."

"That night," Cusik said, "you struck out three times and popped out once."

"Against Cincinnati," Harold agreed softly.

"Right. I was listening on the radio. You guys were heroes, special like nothing else on this earth. And even after that game, I was ready to give you the benefit of the doubt. Because I believed I was going to die. My parents thought so, too. Everybody. It was a desperate time but that night, Harold, I didn't pray for myself. I prayed for you. For *you*, Harold. I was only a kid but I wasn't stupid, I understood how hard it was, that a player couldn't step up and hit a homer whenever he wanted, just because he felt like it or had made a promise. No, there would have to be a special force or inspiration! A higher power at play, intervening in a shitty world where kids like me lay in St. Jude's listening to ball games on the radio, where, for an instant, they got granted grace. Hope prevailed! And even after you struck out three times and popped up—I was praying on every at bat! every pitch!—I told myself that God must have a reason, that the game was still part of his plan, and the grace would come later, another game. So I prayed for you, Harold. You were my link. But the next night you didn't play. Or the night after that, or the night after that. You never played again! I was putting God on your case, Harold, but you didn't even bother to show up."

Harold shook his head.

"You don't know."

He had no precise recollection of what he'd promised the young Cusik. He'd seen a bunch of kids. And he'd completely forgotten that the hospital visits coincided with that game which, among the thousands in his career, still gnawed at his being.

❁

The season hadn't started badly. Harold played well in May, but he tapered off in July, and by August he was in a dreadful slump. He didn't panic, though, because he was a veteran of five seasons, he'd seen ups and downs, and he knew that at times like these, you had to trust your skills to do their work. He and Kimberly had just moved into a big new house on Windemere Bluffs and she flew back and forth with a group of friends on pleasure trips to Miami. It was perfectly fine—he was a millionaire, after all. He still had another year on his contract, and then he'd be a free agent. Arnie Swanson told him, "Harold, I'm looking forward to that bidding war!"

But the slump. Hitless for four straight games, and the previous week had been almost as bad. He was getting nervy, made a couple of errors in the outfield. That night against Cincinnati, with Fisher on the mound, he terribly needed some hits. He had no fear of Fisher. He knew he could touch this guy.

His first time at bat, he swung and a foul tip grazed his ankle. A stupid little accident, but painful. He stepped out of the box to walk it off, then stepped back in. Harold was concentrated, in the moment, and he didn't think to call a time-out and ask the trainer to look at it.

To this day, he couldn't say if it mattered. If he started favoring this ankle, if it threw off his timing. (Years later, he'd made numerous drunken phone calls to ex-teammates, claiming as much, but honestly he didn't know if it was true.) He'd had other injuries, broken fingers and inflamed joints, and he'd played through them. To get this far, you had to be tough. But for that night, he didn't know.

Three successive strike-outs. Then, in the bottom of the eighth inning, his final at bat. There were two men on base. His team trailed by a run. With a hit, he could tie the game. A long ball could win it. He faced a relief pitcher, a left-hander he'd never seen before. On the second pitch, he connected perfectly: a line shot soared toward the left field seats. The instant the ball struck his bat, he could feel it in his hands: oh, the sweet spot! Before he had time to look up, he knew that this one was *gone*.

A roar! But at the last instant the ball twisted foul, narrowly missing the pole. A groan, from thousands. Harold trotted back to the batter's box, where he worked through a few more pitches before popping up to the left side of the infield. They lost the game.

The next day, the manager benched him and put in Sanford Dupree, a lanky rookie from Texas. Dupree got two hits, so the manager left him in the line-up for another game. He got another hit and the following day, he whacked two home runs. Harold spent the last month of the season on the bench while Dupree went on a tear.

During this time Harold took extra batting practice, consulted the trainer about his ankle; he wanted to recover his old timing but in order to do so, he needed the opportunity, a chance to play regularly and get into a rhythm. Instead he was relegated to pinch hitting, an unpredictable role that destabilized him. Each attempt put everything on the line. In eight at bats that final month, he managed only a sacrifice fly. Harold had trouble sleeping at night, worrying about the next day. In late innings where it appeared he might get summoned, he also had to duck back to the clubhouse and sit on the toilet, his bowels gone entirely liquid.

Over the long winter he was haunted by that game against Cincinnati, particularly by his mighty stroke that had narrowly missed the pole. Just inches! What if the ball hadn't twisted foul? He would've broken his slump! Won the game! In such circumstances, the manager wouldn't have benched him the next day. He would've regained his confidence and recovered his stride. Sanford Dupree—that fucker—would still be a guy nobody had heard of, instead of the new sensation and a pretext for journalists' exaggerations. That winter Harold often drank late into the night calculating the team payroll and calling Arnie Swanson about Arnie's theory that the front office would sell Dupree to another team to raise some quick cash. Arnie had speculated about this only once but Harold made him repeat it many times.

During spring training, Dupree was still with the team, wowing onlookers. Even when the kid made a mistake, got fooled by a pitch, somehow his puny pop fly fell into the hole. Harold watched and felt his head would explode. On the field, Harold performed miserably. He stayed sober the entire time—threw himself fearlessly into two-a-day workouts—but he couldn't pull his game together. At the end of March, he was cut from the roster and sent down to the minors. The money still flowed in, because there remained a year on his contract, but his pride was shattered. He abandoned the Des Moines team mid-season and took a Mediterranean vacation with Kimberly and a group of their friends. He danced in Ibiza, ate sea urchins in Nice, and he enjoyed many bottles of pinot gris. "I'll be a free agent," he told Kimberly. "I'll sign with a new team." When he came back to the U.S., Arnie Swanson told him, "You're radioactive, man. Who's gonna touch you now?"

"I tried to put you out of my mind," Cusik was saying. "And I did, because you, Harold, are utterly insignificant. I had bigger worries, believe me. But what a coincidence, all these years later! When I saw that name on the payroll—Harold Hines— I wondered, could it be *my* Harold Hines? There aren't that many Hines, I suppose, and how many of them are Harolds? So I looked into your case. And it *was* you. Behold the man! I found out many things about you. And that's why I wanted this conversation. I have questions, I'm curious about your insights. Truly. How about this question: looking back on it all, is there anyone, I mean *anyone*, who sucks more than you?"

"Listen," Harold said, "I'm sorry I disappointed you that day. I shouldn't have made that promise. It was foolish of me. We were just trying to cheer you up."

"Let me show you something, hot shot." Grasping for his crutches, Cusik struggled to his feet, moved around his desk.

"But surely you understand now," Harold continued. "Baseball isn't for kids. The pressure in that business! It isn't about winning, not really. Because winning never lasts. You just try to survive while everybody else is waiting for you to fail, *hoping* you'll fail, because it'll allow them to hang on and survive a little bit longer."

Cusik poked Harold's chair with a crutch. "Stop whining, it's embarrassing. What do you know of the world of pain? Look over here."

With a sigh, Harold rose and followed him to a corner of the office, where Cusik balanced himself before a frame on the wall. From a distance, Harold had assumed it was a painting but closer up he saw two narrow pieces of leather, mounted on a velvet background.

"See those?" Cusik asked.

"Uh huh."

Cusik tilted his head appreciatively, while Harold wondered what he was supposed to say. He definitely preferred the ceramic avocado in the waiting area.

"Do you ever think about Providence, Harold? I've always envied Jean-Jacques Rousseau in *The Confessions*. I bet you would, too."

"How so?"

"He'd been full of doubts about the universe. It tortured Rousseau, really. Well, one day he was throwing stones and he made a test. He couldn't stand it anymore, because he needed answers! So he took aim at a tree. He told himself, 'If I hit the tree, all is well with God and I will go to heaven. If I miss, there is no hope in my existence and I am damned.' He threw the stone, and there was a terrible moment of not knowing. He had to wait in order to see. But the stone found its target. Hit the tree. After that day, he said he knew he would be all right. He never again worried about his fate."

"Sounds like he was a pitcher," Harold said.

"Go ahead and joke. You could say it's a lot of romantic nonsense. But consider a child with a degenerative disease of the spinal column who might never walk again, whose very survival is in doubt. What was God's intention for him? Was he supposed to be content that he could still move his toes? Was he wrong to long for more? He, too, needed a sign. And then Harold Hines appears and announces he'll step up to the plate for him."

"Not like that," said Harold.

"You volunteered it, not I."

"Not like that!"

"In the end, you took God away from me. Should I thank you?"

"Hold on. That's not on me. You had to throw your own stones."

"I haven't done too badly. You see, my condition was considered too risky for titanium implants, such surgeries would finish me. That's what everyone said. And then I got my first leg braces—talk about a contraption—freakin' Victorian! Nobody thought I'd ever walk. But I'm stubborn, Harold. I worked those babies so hard, I actually wore them out. Look at those boot-straps." He nodded toward the frame. "I pulled so hard they broke!"

He threw back his head and laughed, a deep, almost bovine rumble from his narrow chest, ending in a wheeze. Then he clumped back to the other side of his desk, swiveled and sat down. He dropped the crutches and poured himself another glass of scotch. "Sure you don't want one?"

Harold shook his head.

Cusik sniffed his glass. He sipped, his forehead wrinkling, and licked his lips. "*Oooh*. Nice!"

"You do like a show, don't you?"

"Thank you, Harold. But I won't dance. Just so you know. Please sit down. Please? There now. Shall we get back to business? That's what we're here for. Am I to understand that you refuse a promotion? You're turning down this job?"

"That's right."

"You would keep your current job instead?"

"That's right. I told you why."

"Harold Hines—a big league dishwasher!"

Harold blinked slowly, then closed his eyes for several seconds. "I've done things I regret, but I'm not going to apologize for that." He opened his eyes.

Cusik stared back at him, his chin propped on a fist.

"My my. Mr. Hines will not be brushed back. Tell me, Harold, when you were a child, did you ever do experiments with insects? They're so small, you're like God, really. Did you ever kill a bug, just for the hell of it? Squash it?"

There was a juicy quality in Cusik's voice. He wasn't good at holding his liquor.

"Yes, I suppose I did."

"OK, Harold." Cusik took another sip. "Watch me!" He put down the glass. With his thumb, he made a squashing gesture on his desk. "Oooh, sorry!" He paused, turning his thumb back and forth. "Does that hurt? Sorry, Harold!" He continued grinding his thumb. "You're not even a dishwasher anymore." Cusik stopped and looked up. "You're fired."

Instantly Harold rose to his feet. Ready to tell him to fuck off, he quit this job. He would slam the door.

But then he saw something unexpected in Cusik's eyes, a glitter of rebellion. It struck him as ridiculous and as he glared back, trying to make sense, the power shifted. No—he would not leave this office. Why should he? He would do as he pleased. Without a word Harold slowly walked around the desk.

With his forearms, Cusik lifted himself up out of his chair. His face was fearful but he was no coward, his jaw thrust out as he stood quivering. Harold ignored him and bent down and scooped up the crutches. He didn't even have to think about it. He continued to the window, turned the handle and opened it. He threw the crutches out the window.

Down, down they fell. From the height of the 18th floor he had time to watch their descent with a horrified satisfaction. Like wings ripped off a body, useless. One crutch landed in the bushes, the other bounced off and skittered onto the sidewalk. Fortunately no one was walking by.

"My, how impressive you are!"

Harold turned around, suddenly aware of the pounding of his heart. If only this day could start over. He regretted coming here. Cusik teetered slightly. With the smallest shove, Harold could push him over. With a puff of breath, it seemed. Cusik looked unhappy but also expectant. Did he want Harold to finish the job? Was that it? But Harold couldn't do it. He felt ashamed of what he'd created.

"This is messed up," he said.

"Now go fetch them for me, Harold. Jump."

Cusik laughed but Harold couldn't tell if it was another of the man's strange jokes or if he really meant it, that's what he wanted to see. Harold went back to the window and pushed it shut.

As he did so, he noticed a tow truck in the parking lot below, raising the front wheels of his Toyota.

The sight gave him a queer feeling. Not even Cusik would be able to arrange such a perfectly-timed intervention. The tow truck began to pull away. Harold turned around.

"I better go. Take care of yourself."

"Where are you going?"

Harold took the elevator down to the lobby, and then left the building and surrounding shrubs. There was no foot traffic out here. Soon he walked alone down the highway, cars buzzing past.

TEN

Jordan County, 2022

Antediluvian

Paul had never forgiven him. And now, a phone call out of the blue.

It came when his son was displaying his mental prowess. Milo announced that he'd memorized the periodic table of elements. He handed his father a photocopy. "OK," Paul said. "Go." Milo began to recite: "Hydrogen, helium, lithium, beryllium . . ." He reeled off the first fifty correctly before he hesitated, his face clouding. "Osmium?" Paul shook his head. "You skipped a couple. Take your time." Milo clenched his jaw and squinched his eyes. Paul could almost hear a crackle of synapses.

"Iridium?"

"No, sorry."

Milo squeezed his fists to his temples—and then Paul's phone rang.

"Gaaah!" His son threw out his arms.

"But that was impressive," Paul said, ignoring the ringtone. "You got most of them."

"Leave me alone!"

Milo stomped out of the room.

Paul answered his phone.

"Did you see? We're on the news!"

No, he certainly wasn't expecting this call. For the last 22 years, he'd avoided speaking to this man. When Bobby identified himself, Paul was momentarily at a loss. He blinked at the periodic table.

"What news?"

"Local—channel seven. They found our drawing in Carson Cave. It's a sensation! This might be our best stunt yet."

"Huh? I don't have anything to say to you. How did you get my cell number?"

"Come on, Doctor Big Shot. Whether you like me or not, we'd better figure out how to handle this. We need a strategy."

"I don't know who 'we' is."

"I'll send you a link."

Years ago, to celebrate victory in a high school baseball game, they'd gone to Carson Cave to drink beer. Bobby had stolen a cooler. His technique was brazen, targeting an unattended picnic table when its occupant was distracted by a child near the boat dock. Bobby swooped in and grabbed the cooler and exited without breaking a stride. The operation took three or four seconds. Then, avoiding the road, he descended a footpath to the river.

"Timing," he said, popping a beer. "That's all it is."

Paul nervously kept watch on the path, near the mouth of the cave. Bobby claimed to have discovered the place himself, though Paul didn't believe him. At sunset the light angled into the entrance and gave the stone a golden glow. The mouth of the cave wasn't visible from the path but they kept their voices low. Bobby had thrown down a pair of sleeping bags to make it comfortable. He called it Carson Cave because his last name was Carson and he wanted to take credit.

Tonight, they were in the grip of a buzz, even before they started drinking. Paul had pitched a hard-fought game and

Bobby, playing second base, had contributed two hits. It was impossible to go home before they'd processed their victory and analyzed its twists and turns. Not everyone appreciated why this was necessary. Paul's parents assumed he would win while Bobby's parents had no time for trivial things like baseball. They stayed home to care for his sister.

"I'd like to live here," Bobby said, admiring his cave. "If I could hook up a TV, I would."

Paul laughed. His friend still indulged in little boy fantasies, and he wasn't embarrassed to admit it. Maybe Bobby half-believed his words.

Bobby picked up a rock and scratched on the wall. "Look at you, man." A crude figure emerged, its arm flung back. At first, Paul assumed it was a depiction of himself, pitching, but Bobby kept scratching and the arm grew longer, thicker: it was a bat.

Next he sketched another figure, a woman of exaggerated voluptuousness, her arm extended. She was the pitcher.

As a final touch, he added an oversized penis to the batter.

"You and Frances," Bobby said.

"Jesus, Bobby. That's just stupid. Grow up."

"Think you can do a better job?"

Before the light faded, Bobby sketched in extra touches and details—a campfire, an orb sailing in the air. He worked fast, accidentally discovering that another rock, moistened with spilled beer, allowed him to add red highlights. Paul found a similar stone and helped out, embellishing his figure, making himself taller. The drawing acquired a goofy charm as they became immersed, acting on each other's suggestions.

Then it got too dark and they finished a twelve-pack, listening to the river.

❁

The link to channel seven news included a story about the discovery of ancient cave paintings near the Reed River. Authorities had been alerted and the site was sealed off. A paleontologist at the local university said it was evidence of a prehistoric community in the area. "This will oblige us to rethink our timeline and our understanding of migration patterns."

Good Lord, Paul thought. Is there anything people won't swallow?

He didn't bother to return Bobby's call, but the next day, when Paul was double-parked outside Monaco's Deli and waiting for his wife Sandra, Bobby called again. "Did you check out the link?"

"Yeah, I saw it."

"You haven't told anyone, have you?"

"Why should I tell anyone? They'll put two and two together. I suspect the old beer cans are a pretty good clue."

"I never left any. I needed the deposit. Listen, Paul, I got a plan—"

"And I don't want to hear it."

Sandra had stepped out of the deli with their carry-out order. Monaco's was overpriced but he and Sandra had put in a long day at Owl Optics and didn't feel like cooking. He shut off his phone. Sandra slid into her seat, smelling of tomato and basil. They drove on to pick up Milo from his guitar lesson.

❁

Back in the cave, he'd been in love with Frances Talucci. He hadn't told a soul, but Bobby had sniffed it out. In those days Frances attended an all-girl Catholic school and was a star pitcher in fast-pitch softball. Ordinarily their paths wouldn't have crossed but one day, during a rain delay, teams playing parallel tournaments at the city park found themselves biding time at a gymnasium. Pitchers were throwing, to keep warm. His eyes lingered on a stocky girl, high-busted, with long curly hair and a wicked underhand delivery. *Smack*. Her velocity was impressive. *Smack*. Others gathered to watch and soon a challenge emerged. "Anyone want to face her in the batting cage?"

No one stepped forward. Oh, Paul's teammates laughed and feigned indifference, but there was a tension in the air, and the reason was obvious. Nobody wanted to get shown up by a girl. *Smack*. Everybody stood around, waiting for somebody else to react. So Paul selected a bat and stepped forward.

She walked up to her mark and gave him a little nod. He nodded back.

A pause, then her arm whipped. He swung and fouled it backward. Barely got a piece of it. Her unfamiliar motion put him off balance.

He felt the gaze of his teammates, how much they were rooting for him, and suddenly the pressure felt greater than in a real game, because this *wasn't* a game: he was representing the guys.

The next pitch he jumped on too early and the ball trickled harmlessly to his left, another foul.

Now she took longer to set up. He was aware of his body, his hunched stance, his exposed, bony wrists. She looked at her glove where she gripped the ball, concentrating, then she lifted her eyes, searching for the right spot. Her arm whipped.

He swung and missed completely.

A few hoots and whistles—oh sure, none of it was serious, was it? Just fooling around in the gym. He gave her a quick wave and replaced his bat in the rack. He went back to resume his throwing, acting very busy.

Soon word came that the weather had cleared and they could go outside again. Everyone gathered up their kit bags. He looked in her direction. She was heading for the door. Then she saw him.

Again, she nodded.

Years later, Paul replayed this moment countless times in his mind, but he couldn't remember what he did next, whether he acknowledged her sign. He was a blank. But she walked straight to him. "Can I talk to you for a minute?"

Paul didn't move. Was she going to gloat?

"Thanks for stepping up," she said.

He laughed nervously. "Not my finest moment."

"I wouldn't say that. None of those other guys is brave enough."

She smiled as if they shared an understanding, and then she walked on. Paul wished he'd said something clever. He was unable to shake the image of her brown eyes and thick hair, her smile, and the jut of her hip as she strode away.

Paul and Sandra were licensed opticians at Owl Optics. They managed a store at the Warehouse, a new commercial center on the site of a former box factory which now hosted start-ups and a World Food Court. Paul and Sandra had built an airy four-bedroom house in Turnball Heights. Their son, Milo, was the best in his group of gifted students. He read Spanish comic books and had already trounced his parents at chess. He still had the table manners of a ten-year old, though, stuffing his mouth with bread till his cheeks bulged and licking Monaco's arrabbiata sauce off his fingers. Later that evening, he surprised Paul by confiding that he was unhappy because another boy had told him that he threw like a girl.

"That's a stupid thing to say," Paul replied. "Ignore him."

"Could you teach me to throw better?"

This was the first time that Milo had expressed such an interest. The garage was full of athletic gear that had gone unused. On vacations Milo preferred to read in the Jacuzzi.

"Sure," Paul said.

They went to the back yard and Paul tried to help him with his motion. Milo was a bit uncoordinated, but that could be addressed. Paul hadn't thrown hard since his freshman year in college, before a rotator cuff surgery had ended his pitching dreams. Now he tossed a gentle, slow overhand, encouraging Milo to learn sound mechanics. There was pleasure in these gestures, as well as an intimation of a larger game, with its difficult and unchanging rules. His phone vibrated in his pocket but he ignored it. Milo wasn't too good at catching the ball, either—it deflected off his glove then bounced off his chin—but he didn't complain or make excuses and another time, he trapped the ball against his chest. "Good one!" Paul encouraged.

Back in the house, checking the phone, he saw that it was Bobby Carson. He put the phone back in his pocket. Later that same evening when Milo was in the bath and Sandra was doing yoga on the back patio, Bobby called again.

"So I got in touch with the professor who was on TV," he announced. "Professor Spivak? Know what he said? He sees a stylistic resemblance in this cave painting to examples from the Upper Paleolithic Era. 'That is my hypothesis,' he said. Fuck, Paul! We could be in *National Geographic*!"

"This can't last. Surely they'll do carbon dating or something."

"Yeah, he did mention that. But for now we're the toast of the town. Since they ran the story, the professor has been contacted by lots of places, it's going on national media. 'Stylistic resemblance!' I must've learned something from Fat Fergie after all."

Bobby's tone, the assumed complicity—it was like a door had opened onto a lost world. As if they were still kids, playing pranks and laughing till their sides hurt. Fat Fergie had been their high school art teacher, an obese man who wore color-ful ties and tried to instill culture with slide-shows. Bobby had gotten kicked out of Mr. Ferguson's class for ad-libbing voices for famous paintings. "Pull my finger," said God on the Sistine Chapel.

"You don't seem to understand," Paul said. "I have no desire to reminisce about Fat Fergie. I don't care about the cave. All that is ancient history."

"I hear you, doctor! I'm talking about *what next*. Remember those guys in England with crop circles? If we're smart, we could play it like that, only bigger. The question is, when is the time to come forward and take credit? How do we capitalize?"

Paul was taken aback. Capitalize? Hang on. Why should his name be linked to this painting? There was his business at Owl Optics to consider, his image in town. The past was full of dumb and regrettable things that a normal person didn't want to re-visit. He had no wish to be associated with something so puerile. "Count me out." He switched off his phone.

Mostly, though, he was thinking about Frances.

☼

Bold—there was no choice but to be bold. Since Frances at-tended a different school, there weren't any built-in social oppor-tunities or courtship situations. They would never cross paths. So he had to seek her out and assert his presence.

He went to one of her games, and then another, watching contests between unfamiliar teams—a spy in a strange land—

watching *her*. And with astonishing ease he learned all about Frances, the way she carried herself in public, interacted with teammates, expressed joy or frustration. He spent a lot of time studying her short, curvy body, the lines of the uniform, her compact power. He even met her family, because the grandstand was full of Taluccis. Brothers and sisters, her curly-haired mom and bald dad, and another bald man, a big-mouthed uncle who bellowed, "Go-oo-oo, Franny!" There were so many Taluccis that Paul wondered about the transportation arrangements, if they had their own bus.

This was her world. So very different from Paul's. He had no siblings and his parents, though supportive, were too busy to attend his games. His father's dental practice was booming and his mother played competitive bridge at high levels and attended her own tournaments. Maybe that fact had brought him closer to Bobby, whose parents had other priorities than baseball, too. The Carsons ran a heating and air-conditioning business. Bobby's father was always out in the van for an installation or a repair, while his mother managed the office and Bobby was expected to help with his little sister, Judy, who was a child with Down syndrome. Sometimes you'd see Bobby and Judy in front of the office downtown, on a bench near a traffic light, watching the world roar by, Judy licking an ice-cream.

One Saturday, after seeing Frances strike out the last batter and win her game, Paul hurried down to the front row by the first-base line, where she would see him as she left the field.

"Good job!" he called.

She appeared surprised but she walked straight to him.

"What are you doing here?"

"I came to see you."

"That right?" She smiled, and he felt a lightness such as he'd never known. As if he'd entered a new territory where shyness and limitations no longer signified. He could be frank and honest, because the only currency was hope.

"I need to talk to you, Frances. I need to see you."

"Like, *now?*"

She was still in uniform, dusty from the game, and in seconds they were surrounded by her family and friends who came to congratulate her. Suddenly he realized that she didn't even know his name. "I'm Paul."

❀

"Who was that on the phone?" Sandra asked, rolling up her yoga mat. She wore iridescent purple leggings.

"I was talking to Bobby Carson."

"Really? I thought you didn't like that guy. Is he trying to sell you something?"

"Yeah. That's it."

It wasn't exactly a lie. Bobby had become a real estate agent and you saw his face on signs all over town. That's how Sandra knew about Paul's antipathy toward Bobby. Once, stopped at a red light, he noticed a sign and exclaimed, "Jesus, will that asshole ever go away?"

"But we don't want to buy anything," she said.

"That's what I told him."

Sandra had gone to school in a St. Paul suburb, so she knew nothing about what had happened. They'd met in an optometrics course and settled here after they got married. Over the years, he'd never lied to Sandra. But he'd never mentioned Frances Talucci, either.

☼

The first Saturday the young couple went to see a movie; the following weekend they watched the finals of a girls softball tournament. Paul much preferred their second date because unlike in the theater, where chase scenes and exploding fireballs occupied their attention, in the grandstands they could talk. Frances wore sandals, her toenails painted crimson—he often glanced at her small brown hands and feet, trying not to stare at her body—and she told him her opinions about umpires and last week's movie and why she was going to college to be a teacher and a coach. Paul told her of his plans to be a doctor. Frances seemed at ease with him though Paul noticed that she was also chatty with spectators in nearby seats and with the guy who sold peanuts. Maybe it had something to do with being from a big family. People didn't spook her.

When they left the game, she took his hand on their way to the parking lot. They kissed when they said goodnight, which was both encouraging and bittersweet because the next day he was leaving town for two weeks to join his parents on vacation. When he came back, summer would be over, they would return to their different schools and seeing each other would become difficult. Paul had begged his parents to let him stay behind, but they would hear nothing of it.

For two weeks Paul punished his parents in their cabin by a lake in northern Wisconsin by making a point of not enjoying himself. His father Mitch considered these retreats as a sacred, manly ritual, fishing and hiking in a favorite pair of old lace-up boots, far away from his dental practice, from TV and telephones; Paul's mother, Connie, sunned on the dock, drinking rosé, her nose in a book. Paul spent his time moping indoors where he composed moony letters to Frances. One day, Paul and his father argued about starting a fire. Mitch prided himself on using only one match. If you arranged the chips and kindling correctly, one match was all it took. Mitch had explained his method and demonstrated its success. "See—just one." He smiled, pleased with his skill. This time Paul was preparing the chimney and he noticed that his father was observing closely, and he became aware that his father's opinion of him was at stake. Would he manage with only one match? Paul slowed down, giving his father an opportunity to look away or go do something else. But no, his father still watched him. A sudden intuition flowed through Paul that somewhere in the man's heart was a place, a place that maybe he didn't even realize existed, that would be *glad* if Paul failed. That way he would remain secure in his superiority.

With a grunt Paul seized a can of lighter fluid and carelessly doused the wood, struck several matches with a lazy swipe and tossed them on the pile. An audible clap—whoosh!—a huge gust of flame. Paul jumped back from the chimney. "The hell is the matter with you?" his father cried, stomping his boot.

Upon returning from vacation, he telephoned Frances but she was no longer available. "The truth is," she said, "I've started seeing someone else, and it wouldn't be appropriate. I'm sorry."

Paul was gutted. He blamed his parents. This wouldn't have happened if he'd stayed in town! And he was even less prepared for what came next. He assumed his rival was someone from Frances' circle, someone he didn't know. But a few months later, he gripped Bobby in a headlock and demanded to know if the rumors were true.

"I didn't mean to!" Bobby squirmed like a puppy. "We'd go to the cave and hang out. Her parents are strict as hell, there's no question of an abortion. That's what they say. My mom and dad are totally pissed and they say I have to step up to the plate."

To Paul's amazement, Bobby expected his pity.

"There's no way out, man!" he said. "Sometimes I want to kill myself."

☼

"He's a dirtbag," Paul told Sandra. "That's why I don't like him. See, I knew a fellow in high school, a nice guy, he had a girlfriend and Bobby wormed his way in and next thing you know, he gets her pregnant. Big-time stupid. Maybe it sounds like a cliché but it's more than that. There were major consequences. This girl was a sweet kid, plenty of potential, the world was her oyster. And what happens is, she doesn't even finish high school, she wrecks her life to marry a jerk like Bobby and they have three kids, bang-bang-bang, before they turn around and get divorced and she has a bunch of other problems. A lot of grief. But Bobby's face is still smiling all over town. He's remarried with a new wife half his age. OK, maybe ten years younger, I shouldn't exaggerate. But that's what I hear. The guy is always seeking attention and it gets under my skin."

Sandra waited a few seconds. "It was your girlfriend, wasn't it?"

Paul sighed, feeling lame. Was he that obvious? "Right. It was a million years ago and all very small-time. We barely dated. I feel silly even talking about it."

"That was the woman we saw in Crap Palace, wasn't it?"

Now he was startled. How did Sandra pick up on *that?* It was almost clairvoyant, creepy.

Of course, the store wasn't really called Crap Palace. That's just how they referred to it, a vast and ugly retail outlet on the edge of town. Paul and Sandra generally avoided the place and would never consider it for food shopping but occasionally stopped by to stock up on cleaning products and other household crap. They got in and out as fast as they could. One Saturday, Paul was barreling along with a trolley stacked as high as his head with paper towels. Sandra was off somewhere filling her trolley with tiki torches and mosquito repellent candles. Milo had parked himself on a bench in Customer Service where he listened to a podcast on the Galapagos Islands. (He had a thing about turtles.) A slow-moving trolley ahead of Paul forced him to slow down. A woman dawdled in front of a pyramid of canned chili. It was Frances.

"Paul?"

"Well, hello."

His mind raced as they faced each other in the grainy blue fluorescent light. Frances was still pretty, but her cheeks were puffed out as if she was wearing a mask of herself that didn't fit quite right. Her eyes were smaller. She was fat, too. He didn't want to think these thoughts, but he did.

"You must've made quite a mess," she remarked.

For a moment Paul was bewildered, and then he remembered his mountain of paper towels.

"A huge one!" he agreed.

She flashed a smile and he knew, *oh he knew*, how glad he was to see her. Years of stored-up feeling washed over him. He didn't know where it came from, it was strange, and he could only suppose that it had always been there. They chatted and, without mentioning Bobby Carson, she told him about her kids. The eldest, Robby, had graduated from high school three years ago and now worked a night shift at this very store. Paul could've said, *I heard a couple of years ago he was mixed up in a drug bust. Glad to know he's not in jail.* Her middle child, Kaylee, she told him, was in the navy, presently stationed in Yokosuka, Japan. Paul could've replied, *When I was snooping on the Internet for information about you I found hardly anything except your DUI arrests but there were a lot of selfies of Kaylee who unfortunately doesn't resemble you.* Her youngest child, Garth, she said, was a high school senior. "Talk about a handful, let me tell you!"

Paul shivered. The air-conditioning at Crap Palace was always cranked to full-blast. This place was like a slaughterhouse.

"Somebody's waving at you," she said.

He turned and saw Sandra at the end of the aisle. Her trolley was full. Tall in her jodhpur slacks, a silk scarf around her neck, she gave a quick thumbs up and pushed on toward the checkout.

"That your wife?" Frances asked.

"Yes."

"She's elegant."

"Yes, she is. Well, it was great talking to you."

That was months ago. Sandra hadn't said a word that day. But she'd remembered, and now she'd instantly made the connection to Bobby Carson. So why not confide the rest?

"Even if it was an immature teenage thing, I still wonder what she saw in him. It surprises me to this day. Bobby was a conniver. A weasel. I'm being objective here. What did he have to offer?"

Sandra laughed.

"Sometimes it's less what a guy has to offer than what he's ready to forget. For instance, scruples."

"He pretended he was my friend."

She shrugged. "Well, to be fair, he didn't act alone. You might think you're being gallant to stand up for your old sweetheart, but she made her choices, too."

Paul listened, he couldn't contradict her, exactly, but there was something incomplete or even patronizing in her description. No, it wasn't that simple. It was more complicated in the cave.

❉

"Hey, doctor. How's it going?"

Paul raised his gaze from his computer screen. Bobby looked around the shop, all gleaming chrome and reflecting glass. There were no other customers, and he sat down across from Paul.

"We need to talk. You don't answer my messages."

"Go away, Bobby. I'm working."

"It's still about Franny, isn't it? For fuck's sake. I'd thought you'd moved on. How many years has it been? Just say what you want to say and get it off your chest."

Despite his irritation, Paul was also intrigued, impressed even, at Bobby's approach. Once again he'd called him *doctor*. How did he know about this sore spot? Was it instinct? He could smell a vulnerability and go straight to it?

Paul was no doctor. His father Mitch chuckled at Paul and Sandra's white lab coats, which were part of the value-added strategy of Owl Optics. It made the franchise appear serious while charging more than competitors for the same eyeglass frames made in China. "Cute bird," Mitch said, in reference to the stitched logo of a bespectacled owl on their lab coat pockets. Paul knew the man was thinking (and thereby reminding Paul, whether he wanted to think about it or not) of Paul's struggles in college and his D+ grade in organic chemistry and his abandoning the pre-med program. (Mitch had got an A in organic chemistry—he was actually quite fond of organic chemistry.) Yes, it was all true, Paul wouldn't deny it, though his abandonment of pre-med was many years ago and he felt acutely that this truth fell short of doing justice to his life. When could his father let it go? Or why should a bullshitter like Bobby Carson address him as *doctor?* Paul's feet shuffled convulsively under his desk. *Stop telling me who I am!*

Sandra entered the shop, returning from her lunch break, and she drew up short. Her expression told him that she could see his anger. "Come with me," he told Bobby. It was his turn for lunch. On their way out, Paul made introductions. "This is Bobby Carson. We've got a few things to discuss." Sandra shook Bobby's hand, and Paul watched them size each other up. Bobby's look of approval of Sandra's appearance was irksome. He felt a mad impulse to shove Bobby aside. "Let's go."

The World Food Court at the Warehouse commercial center was a short stroll from Owl Optics. Paul ordered spicy Indonesian noodles and Bobby opted for a fish taco. By the time they sat down with their meals under the atrium, Paul had regained his composure.

"Let's make one thing clear. I have nothing to get off my chest about Frances Talucci. That's all past and done."

"Easy for you to say." Bobby bit into his taco. "I got reamed on the child support by a lady judge." He swallowed. "If I'd done half the drunken shit that Franny pulled before she went on the wagon, I wouldn't even have partial custody. It was pure sexism, dude, and I will call it by its name."

Paul raised a palm. "I don't want to hear this."

"Fine—it's not what I came to talk about anyway. I want to show you these."

Bobby pulled out his phone and began to swipe through photos. "I've been doing some research. Look at that." He leaned forward and swiped. "And look at that. You seeing what I'm seeing?"

It was cave art. Paul had viewed similar images before, if not exactly the same ones. He twisted noodles on a fork, then raised them to his mouth. "What do you want me to say?"

"These are from Spain, they say around 30,000 years old. If you put aside the ones with animals, which I haven't bothered to download here, and focus on the paintings with the people, it's freaky as hell. Look at the people. This blows my mind."

"What?"

Overhead, rain began to patter on the atrium.

"The resemblance, man! There—look at the arm. And there—the stick. *The bat.* They're playing, Paul."

It took a moment for these words to sink in.

"Baseball? That's what you're saying, Bobby? Ancient humans, running around in moss underwear, played baseball?"

"Go ahead and laugh. I didn't say it was baseball like ours. There are variations, you know. Jai alai comes from Basque country. These paintings are from that region, if you look at a map. This makes it more meaningful. Part of something bigger."

Paul ripped open a packet of pepper sauce. "That'll take some explaining. What are you driving at?"

"First, you're a condescending prick. Just so you know. Second, I'm saying there's more to what we did than meets the eye. There we were, two kids fooling around, and without knowing it, we tapped into something deeper. Way deeper. We captured an essence, bro. Here we are . . ." he took another bite of fish taco and then used his taco to make a sweeping motion which took in the World Food Court. Rain drummed on the atrium, competing with the piped jazz music, ". . . but we're connected, sure as we sit here, with the dudes who did *that*." He nodded to the image on his phone. "It's the same shit. It's like they're speaking through us. Makes you think."

"Makes me think you spend too much time on the Internet."

Paul expected another retort. But Bobby assumed a thought-ful air, even pious. "The big picture scares you, doesn't it? But I'm seeing this differently now. When we go public, we need to hit the right note and underline the connections. The cave is for real. It's *ours*, man. It's who we are. It's more than a joke, Paul."

Noodle sauce had dripped on Paul's lab coat, and now he rubbed at it with a paper napkin. "How many times do I have to tell you? Say whatever you want, but leave me out."

"So—I take all the credit. It's only me?"

"It's only you."

✿

The rain abated in the afternoon but hit hard again that night, continuing into the morning. The Fourth Street Bridge was closed for public safety. This made for a longer, circuitous route to take Milo to his guitar lesson. And still the rain didn't stop, there was flooding in the east part of town and in adjoining coun-ties. For a week, logistics were a headache. The Warehouse was eerily quiet. The few shoppers wandered like lost souls haunting the shining storefronts.

Paul didn't hear from Bobby during this time. He spent hours filling out the annual self-assessment report for Owl Optics, about which goals had been met, and which areas needed im-provement. He strained to imagine new goals that didn't echo last year's. Sometimes his mind drifted to his conversation with Bobby, and he wondered: why does he seek my support or re-quire my consent? What's in it for him? Won't the cave be the same without me?

✿

On Sunday morning Paul and Sandra met his parents for breakfast. This was a monthly ritual at a downtown diner.

"I bet this handsome young man wants blueberry pancakes!"

Milo smiled at his grandmother Connie. "That's right."

"And then he'll tell us about his girlfriends," his grandfather
Mitch added huskily. "I betcha he's got lots of girlfriends!" Milo
looked down at the table, momentarily shy.

A woman named Heather served them. She was young and
pretty and parried teasing from Paul's father with zingers of her
own, feigning to flirt. Mitch always insisted on picking up the
check and he informed servers in advance that he *might* leave a
generous tip. The food arrived: eggs and low-carb fruit cups for
the ladies, omelettes and hash browns for the men, while Milo
slathered his pancakes with syrup.

"You're not man enough to finish all that," his grandfather
said. "Those pancakes are going to kick your ass."

Milo giggled.

They conversed briefly about the heavy rains till Milo interrupted the adults to announce that he would recite the periodic
table. Between bites, he rattled it off flawlessly, scarcely taking
time to breathe. His grandparents looked on, concerned but ul-
timately approving.

Then they spoke of summer plans. Paul's father wanted to
take the boy up to the cabin in Wisconsin. Milo had never been
away from his parents for longer than a weekend.

"He'll love it! This boy's no noodle. Why, he'll catch his own
walleye for breakfast every morning. You'd like that, wouldn't
you, Milo?"

Milo nodded slowly. His grandmother stood up, clutching her purse, and excused herself. She didn't say where she was going but Paul knew she was stepping outside for a smoke. Sandra excused herself, too. She would go keep Connie company. Paul's father carried on talking as if Milo wasn't supposed to notice his grandmother's cigarettes, but Milo noticed everything.

"You haven't been up to the lake for a while."

"That's true," Paul acknowledged.

"You should make time."

Paul emptied his coffee cup and put it down on the table. "We'll see."

"Milo," the old man said, "you gotta finish those pancakes. Show who's boss!"

At that moment the server Heather arrived with the check. Paul grabbed it before his father could take it. He stood up. "Come on, Milo. We're out of here."

"Hey, that belongs to me!" exclaimed Mitch.

"Nope." Paul counted out the tip.

"The hell is wrong with you?"

✦

Bobby called the next day.

"Bad news, man."

"What do you mean?"

"It got flooded. The river left the banks and wiped out everything up to the picnic area. So the cave was under water for two days. There weren't resources to protect it, at least that's what Professor Spivak says. The waters have receded and the painting is gone. He's pretty bummed. All he has is a photographic record so his research will have to limit itself to style. He's gonna publish the pictures."

"Didn't you tell him the truth?"

"Not yet."

There was a pause, and Paul pursued, "Are you going to?"

"It's like a legacy, right? Our style, and I want to protect it, include it in the record."

"But it's bullshit."

"It's part of us, man."

Paul said nothing.

"Besides," Bobby continued, "the professor wants real bad to get an article out of this. He says it's for the sake of knowledge. Why disappoint him?"

Paul hung up.

JoJo's was a sandwich shop on the far south side. Paul arrived early and ordered an iced-tea, trying to compose his thoughts. When Frances appeared, she wore a green shawl, and her hair, still long and curly but streaked with gray, fell over her shoulders.

"Well, this was unexpected." She slipped into a chair. "I've got another appointment in half an hour so I don't have much time. What can I do for you?"

The phrase sounded forced. *Another appointment.* As he watched her unwrap her shawl, he doubted these words. Why was she so wary? It was true, though, that Sandra didn't know about this meeting with Frances. He might mention it later. That's what Paul told himself.

"Can I get you an iced-tea? Maybe a sandwich?"

Frances shook her head. "I'm good."

A truck rumbled by, vibrating the windows. She looked at him, waiting.

"I wanted to check in with you," he said. "See how things are going." He tried to sound casual, as if this was something they did periodically.

"I'm fine, Paul. And you? How's your wife? You have a son, right?"

"Everybody's good." He placed his palms on the table. "My boy's doing great but he's getting to the age where he likes to push back."

A week ago, after they'd returned from the diner and Paul had announced in unequivocal terms that Milo would not be joining his grandparents at the cabin, Milo had made a scene. Suddenly he wanted to go to the lake. "I don't get to do anything!" he cried.

"Uh—" Paul groped for an argument. "I need to teach you to swim first."

Milo stalked off to his room and slammed the door. He'd shut himself away every night that week. Sandra was surprised at Paul's decision. "Maybe we should let him go. He doesn't have many friends. He could use some growing up." Paul conceded that Milo spent too much time alone with his tablet. Now, as he picked up his glass of iced-tea, it occurred to him that his son had started masturbating. He put down his glass and looked out the window.

"Funny you suggested this place," Frances said. "I meet here sometimes with Judy."

"Judy?"

"Yeah, you remember Judy. Bobby's sister? We keep in touch."

"Oh, right. How is she?"

"She works part-time at Morrisey's, not far from here. Judy's doing OK. She—" Frances trailed off. "You didn't really know her, did you?"

Paul shook his head, trying to picture Judy as an adult. "Not really."

"I've always liked Judy." Now Frances became very still. "Paul, what can I do for you?"

"It's about the cave. What's happened to it. Has Bobby told you?"

She looked at him blankly.

"What cave?"

"You know—by the river."

Her expression turned into a scowl.

"Why would you bring that up? Why would I be talking to Bobby?"

"Well, you mentioned Judy—"

"That's different. She's like a sister to me but Bobby's not worth my time."

Paul wished he could take back his words, the unwelcome images he'd conjured up, of the cave and old sleeping bags, the design scratched on stone. Did she know that he'd had a hand in the writing on the wall? Paul tried to erase the images.

"Oh, the place got flooded and it was on the news, that's all. Bobby talked to me about it. We're not friends, I don't like him, but the thing is—what I'm trying to say—since he got in touch with me, it brought back so many emotions. I suppose I don't have many friends. I'm awfully busy." Paul felt out of breath, as if he'd been running. "My family is great, I'm lucky there, though it's harder with my parents, my dad is a dick. Anyway, the point is—I'm reaching out. I guess I'm asking you to be my friend. You see?"

"You're acting weird, Paul. Why me?"

"Of course you! Frances, you know I like you. Honestly I'd like to fix this crazy world. We're not kids anymore, right?"

"Right. But why ask me? What do you *want* from me? Ask your wife." She looked at him fixedly, as if searching for the right spot. "Actually, it's not her problem. Ask Bobby. Your dad. You fuckers got some stuff to sort out. Don't come to us. Just do it."

Frances stood up and threw her shawl over her shoulders.

"Please. Can't you wait?"

"You want to fix the world, Paul? Go home."

These stories, sometimes in different form, appeared in the following magazines:

- "The New Garden" (as "Ivan the Terrible Goes on a Family Picnic") in *The Brooklyn Review;*

- "Deadball" in *King Ludd's Rag;*

- "Gertie and the Babe" in *The Doctor T.J. Eckleburg Review;*

- "Heaven" in *Burningword Literary Journal;*

- "Little Boy and the Carp" in *Cagibi;*

- "Antennae" in *The Twin Bill;*

- "Foul" in *South Dakota Review;*

- "Wild West Show" in *Aethlon;*

- "The Promise" in *Litro;*

- "Antediluvian" in *The Opiate.*

Charles Holdefer grew up in Iowa and is a graduate of the Iowa Writers' Workshop and the Sorbonne. He currently lives in Brussels, Belgium.

His short fiction has appeared in many magazines, including *New England Review*, *Chicago Quarterly Review*, *North American Review*, *Los Angeles Review*, *Slice* and *Yellow Silk*. His story "The Raptor" won a Pushcart Prize.

He also writes essays and reviews which have appeared in *The Antioch Review*, *World Literature Today*, *New England Review*, *The Dactyl Review*, *The Collagist*, *New York Journal of Books*, *Journal of the Short Story in English* and elsewhere.

ALSO BY CHARLES HOLDEFER

NOVELS

Don't Look at Me (2022)
Bring Me the Head of Mr. Boots (2019)
Back in the Game (2012)
The Contractor (2007)
Nice (2001)
Apology for Big Rod (1997)

STORIES

Agitprop for Bedtime: Polemic, Story Problems, Kulturporn and Humdingers (2020)
Magic Even You Can Do: By Blast (2019)
Dick Cheney in Shorts (2017)

CRITICISM

George Saunders' Pastoralia: Bookmarked (2018)

www.ingramcontent.com/pod-product-compliance
Lightning Source LLC
Chambersburg PA
CBHW020020030726
47499CB00007B/2199